FEED
THEM
SILENCE

ALSO BY LEE MANDELO

Summer Sons

FEED

THEM

SILENCE

Lee Mandelo

TOR PUBLISHING GROUP

New York

FEED THEM SILENCE

Copyright © 2023 by Lee Mandelo

A Tordotcom Book
Published by Tom Doherty Associates/Tor Publishing Group
120 Broadway
New York, NY 10271

www.tor.com

Tor® is a registered trademark of Macmillan Publishing Group, LLC.

Library of Congress Cataloging-in-Publication Data

Names: Mandelo, Lee, author.
Title: Feed them silence / Lee Mandelo.
Description: First edition. | New York : Tom Doherty Associates, 2023.
Identifiers: LCCN 2022041389 (print) | LCCN 2022041390 (ebook) |
ISBN 9781250824509 (hardcover) | ISBN 9781250824516 (ebook)
Subjects: LCSH: Human-animal relationships—Fiction. | Wolves—Fiction. |
Research—United States—Fiction. | LCGFT: Science fiction. | Novellas.
Classification: LCC PS3613.A5354 F44 2023 (print) |
LCC PS3613.A5354 (ebook) | DDC 813/.6—dc23/eng/20220912
LC record available at https://lccn.loc.gov/2022041389
LC ebook record available at https://lccn.loc.gov/2022041390

Our books may be purchased in bulk for promotional, educational, or business
use. Please contact the Macmillan Corporate and Premium Sales
Department at 1-800-221-7945, extension 5442, or by email at
MacmillanSpecialMarkets@macmillan.com.

First Edition: 2023

Printed in the United States of America

0 9 8 7 6 5 4 3 2 1

FEED
THEM
SILENCE

I

The portable surgery unit hulked at the edge of a tract field, ringed by four-by-fours and a lone Jeep. Sean's environmentally conscious subcompact had given up the ghost a mile out from the GPS coordinates. She left it stuck in a truck-sized rut and trekked the rest of the way in her new pair of Timberlands. Oncoming blisters burned her pinky toes. In the distance, the seam between tree line and farmland marked the outer rim of their wolf pack's territory. Outside of the behemoth medical trailer her lab assistant Alex fiddled with his phone in a camp chair. Generators roared loud enough to mute the birds, and the insects, and anything else alive. Alex hadn't heard her approach either.

"Have they started?" she called out.

He jerked, phone catapulting from his startled fingers. Without breaking stride Sean plucked it from the grass near her feet, still playing a music video. She dropped it onto his outstretched palm and grinned at his mildly reproving expression.

"They've been in there a while. Page 'em and see," he said.

The light on the unit's lift glowed red; surgery in-progress, or about to be. She paged through the walkie-talkie attached to the railing and said, "Hey, Dr. Kell-Luddon here. Apologies for the delay, my car couldn't take the off-roading. Am I too late to scrub in?"

A delay, then an unfamiliar voice replied, "Frances thinks yes, too late. We're underway with the animal. The team can handle it, though, no worries."

"Well, shit." She flopped onto the grass next to Alex's chair, stomped flat for seating where the mobile surgery unit's incursion hadn't churned the earth to sucking mud.

"You would've only been observing anyway," Alex said.

Sean propped her forearms on her knees and flexed to crack her neck, back, hips. The crunchy pop at the base of her skull set off a lancing, residual throb through her temple. She massaged the pink weal of scar tissue, stiff and slick in the midst of the bristled hair growing back around it. The surgical procedure she'd undergone for the project was minimal. Neural intervention for the animal was— more *significant*, as the grant phrased it.

"Which one did we trap, do you know?" she asked.

"Kate, I think," he said.

Sean skimmed through her field observation notes. Kate: adult female approximately four years of age, structural member of the pack, hadn't ranged off on her own or whelped despite sexual maturity—unsurprising, given the brutality of the previous winter. Out of the whole spring litter, the pack had only sustained one pup through the cold months. Sean laid her phone facedown on her knee. The sky overhead yawned blue as glass with the promise of another bad season, but the freeze hadn't come yet. The golden chill of November fields from her teenage years was no more. Even in north Minnesota she wore only a lightweight flannel to keep cool as the warmth of fall staggered on, and on, and on. But each successive cold snap hit harder than the last.

"Are you excited?" Alex asked.

"I don't know," she said. "More curious nerves, I guess."

"Groundbreaking use of advanced technology, affective observational perspectives, cutting-edge conservation," he parroted from the press release, poking her shoulder with each phrase.

"God, shut up." She laughed.

If her project succeeded, she'd be a rock star in the field: publicity, publication, funding ever at her fingertips, name-recognition firmly cemented—assuming her colleagues and recruits did their parts to her specifications. Inside the surgical unit were two of her researchers, two from the field biology team, plus a surgeon and a veterinarian. Disciplinary crossover at its finest, according to everyone but her wife, Riya. While the red light glowed, Sean flicked through videos from the trap-cameras. "Kate" was a rangier female with pale cream belly fur that shaded to smoke, lit with blazes of rust-orange around her ears and snout. The platonic ideal of a gray wolf, though just as underweight as the rest of her pack—one of two wild family groups remaining in the state. Her coat was more brindled than those of her parents or her siblings.

"The light's off," Alex said some time later.

She stood and brushed dirt off her jeans as the unit's bay cranked open with a garage-door grind. Charles Grant stood with his surgical-booted feet level with Sean's chin, peering down from the top of the lift.

"Step on, doc," he said.

Sean mounted the lift platform and bounced her heel as it raised ponderously. The surgical unit's central hub housed a desktop computer and a set of imaging readout monitors, a few cabinets, and a single entry into the containment/prep room. Through there, she assumed, waited their wolf. Charles's hands were freshly washed and damp when he shook hers, but his scrubs still carried a fine mist of blood. He'd worn her blood the same way, a few weeks back.

"The neural mesh slid right into place, as expected. June is wrapping now with sutures and cleanup, so you should be able to release her in the morning," he said.

"No complications?"

"None at all. Easy sedation and easy surgery, though she'll be a bald doggie for a little while," Charles said.

As Charles sat at the computer, she ducked into the prep room to scrub up. *Bald doggie*. Sean's matching shave had read as a fashion statement with her already close-cropped hair. Despite all the buzzwords she'd deployed in the cash flow application about *becoming in-kind* with an animal, the slim differentiation in practice—the same surgeon inserting her neural receiver and the wolf's transmitter—remained unsettling. The secure door opened and her mixed team trickled out, eyes smiling over sterile masks. Sean slipped by to greet the veterinarian who stayed behind, then paused on the threshold.

On trail cameras a gray wolf could pass for an oddly colored husky or shepherd mix, long of leg and broad of jaw. But in the flesh, her barrel chest rising and falling at the pace of the ventilator tube lodged between her teeth, Kate filled the room. The furry triangle ears and narrow snout reminded Sean of her own dog, Miller, but the paws—lax and spread with one hanging off the edge of the table—were almost the same size as her wife's hands. Sean wrestled with the urge to stroke the wiry gloss of her coat.

"Impressive, huh," Dr. June said, stripping her gloves off into the trash.

"She's so big," Sean muttered.

The imposing physical reality of her subject flung her imagination back to childhood, the solitary library nook where she devoured books about girls raised by wolves, girls running with the pack—and later, in a fancier library hundreds of miles away, books about women who studied them. Through all her funding applications, public and private alike, Sean had held the significance of her first flush of attraction close and quiet, burrowed ventricle-deep and thereby protected from the rest of the gamesmanship. Nonetheless, June gave her a knowing glance.

"You can pet her, just stay away from the head," she said.

"Am I that obvious?" Sean asked.

"Nah, everyone wants to handle her."

Sean laid a loose palm on the wolf's radiator-warm haunch. The fur was coarser than she expected; her fingers sank deep to scritch. The meat-and-disinfectant stink of surgery combined with stale breath and wet dog. Sean's stomach roiled. At the base of Kate's skull, stitches and suture-tape formed a puckered black-and-purple mouth.

"We were able to ease the mesh in with minimal disturbance to bone and tissue, so honestly, she should be good to go. I'll apply a sealant film over the stitches in an hour or so, then cover that with a patch to keep her from chewing them," June said.

"And if she wakes up fine tomorrow, we release her?" Sean confirmed.

Dr. June hummed her agreement, leading Sean from the room where the wolf remained unconscious—waiting to be cleaned up and put to rights. A shiver of secondhand vulnerability tripped across Sean's nerves. Though she'd been sedated all to hell and stuck in a surgical vise to keep her still, at least she'd been alert for her procedure. Kate lay dead to the world. On the cusp of the anteroom, she cast another backward glance at the lonely animal on the cold steel table; unaware of her hesitation, June said, "Once she's loose you're free to turn your magic machine on."

1 year prior

The popping sizzle of paneer crisping was muffled by the lid of the sauté pan. Jaunty blue apron bows at the first notch of Riya's spine and the dip of her waist contrasted her rigid posture. Sean laid her face in her hands, grant paperwork exploded across the kitchen table, and said, "I'm sorry, hon, but you know the deadline is tomorrow."

Without turning Riya replied, "I'd like to enter into the record that, miraculously, I have kept our date nights free of my students, my grading, and *my* proposals for sixteen months running."

"I appreciate you," Sean said.

Riya snorted. The rising household tension provoked by her workload over the past few months had become palpable, but private grants were the last shot for funding her sure-to-be groundbreaking project. Failing to secure institutional support stung. She was asking for a fairly astronomical sum to pilot a neural linkage between the bodyminds of human and animal to—how had she phrased it?— *approach a shared understanding* of the fears, drives, and desires of one of the last remaining wild packs in the American north. Surely, Riya could understand how toothsore those rejections had left her— but regardless, Sean acknowledged defeat and scooped the printed emails from her intended teammates, photos of rangy wolves, and field notes into a messy stack.

As she crossed the living room to the hall, she patted their fluffy herding dog where he lay on the couch watching muted cartoons. His tail flopped a lazy two-beat in response. In their shared office, her whole worktop was covered in detritus; she added the fresh pile on top. A kitschy HERS & HERS sign hanging from their bookshelf split the room. Riya's side stayed neat, besides the travel knick-knacks on all available surfaces, but Sean's had become a graveyard of La Croix cans and teetering paper. Maybe in the fall term she'd be able to bribe a TA to organize her research hoard.

"Food's ready," Riya shouted from the kitchen.

Sean returned to paneer fried with chiles, tomato, and greens alongside a steaming bowl of rice. Riya dropped into a seat, apron-less, button-up's sleeves rolled to the elbow and incongruous paired with her love-busted sweatpants. Miller's toenails clacked on the floor as he took his customary spot on his bed in the corner, alert to the possibility of misplaced food. Silence dragged on for a minute too long while neither woman moved to start eating.

"I *am* sorry," Sean volunteered, once it became clear she needed to.

"I just—we've talked about this shit. You know how I feel," Riya said.

"We agreed to reserve time, and I keep fucking that up, yeah. I'm the worst."

Riya poked at her dinner. "I'm your wife, but I'm not your *wife*, you understand?"

A refrain Sean had heard, filed for future consideration, and promptly forgotten multiple times in recent months. The first bite of the paneer, savory and well-spiced, filled Sean's mouth with warmth. She groaned. Her partner was a great cook, no doubt about that. And despite the initial tension, Riya's stiff spine had begun to melt by degrees. Wrinkles peeked at the corners of her eyes, the ghost of a smile that hadn't quite formed, as she absorbed Sean's vocal appreciation of the meal.

In further peace offering, Sean said, "I'm turning the files in tonight, double-checking the confirmation tomorrow morning at the office, and then it's done."

Riya tapped her fork on the edge of her bowl. The *tink-tink* perked Miller's ears, tufts bouncing.

"What are your chances for this grant?" she asked.

Sean said, "Honestly, good. Between me, my team, and our signers-on in bio, I think we've got a solid mix. And corporate types love to bankroll science with a feel-good vibe."

"I wouldn't argue that a team with no social scientists, people in sustainability, or ethicists is particularly mixed. And spying on the brains of some starving animals sounds more horror movie than heart-warmer to me," Riya said.

"Hey now," Sean rebuffed. "You know what I'm doing and you know *why* I'm doing it. At least with my project they're funding conservation instead of lobbying for a drilling extension in the Arctic. Or, like, trying to build a sex robot."

Riya pursed her lips. "For some measure of the word conservation, darling. I'm sure they're just as interested in the environment as they are the proprietary opportunities for your team's brain-fuckery, which will have *nothing* to do with VR porn."

Sean swallowed another mouthful of sauce-thick rice.

"Does it matter what motivates them, if their pocketbooks are open?"

"Of course it does," Riya replied, fully frowning. "And you can call those wolves collaborators or 'mutual subjects' all you like, you're still using them as objects of study. Which is, well, *whatever*, but it's gross to pretend anything otherwise."

"That's what you think about my whole field, the subject-object power dynamic stuff. But that doesn't mean we aren't producing good and important data—"

Riya interrupted, "Focusing all your resources on these individual animals to determine what makes them *so special* distracts people from addressing the systems that killed all the other goddamn wolves in the first place, but we've had that argument before too."

Sean closed her jaws around her canned venture-funding interview responses, things like, *observing the behavior of the animal is insufficient without understanding of the interior being.* The truth was, she still chased the same curious desires she'd first nursed as a kid streaming the defunct Animal Planet channel, filling the empty house with chatter while her mom was out working, or playing, or whatever else she did besides parenting. What was it really like to be a wolf among a pack, running freely with constant, unguarded companionship?

As the years rolled on, Sean built herself a real life—hollow spaces spackled over with top degrees, a respectable career, and a marriage that made her colleagues jealous—but the dreaming, the longing, stayed steady. No one could show her what it was like, aside from the animals themselves, and finally she had access to the tools, the opportunity, to *see.*

So for what felt like the four hundredth time since she and Riya first fell out over her proposal and her failure to clean the bathroom, she said, "Won't the becoming-wolf part get people to care more about the systemic problems, like, in a literal emotional sense? I'll be experiencing, for the first time on earth, another creature's thinking, feeling self from the inside. You're constantly talking about how useful stories are for building empathetic understanding—isn't this project a sort of storytelling together with the animal, for everyone else?"

Riya snapped her teeth clean through a bite of paneer. The interior flesh showed cream-pale, held aloft on her fork. One fat red drop of sauce plopped onto her plate. Silence settled across the table; gingery greens stuck in Sean's throat as she swallowed. Whenever her wife paused to organize a full response, the outcome wasn't going to be good. She'd taken delight in watching her dissect other people's flawed arguments more times than she could count; having the brilliant edge turned on her was less pleasant.

Collected and precise, Riya said, "If the fact that we're destroying every habitat on this godforsaken planet hasn't stuck with the corporations whose money you're begging for by now, then you doing some brain-in-a-jar bullshit to say how a wolf feels about *dying* won't matter either. This wolf can't consent to being studied by you, which involves a nonconsensual surgical procedure. The presumption you're making in claiming to report on its real feelings, so you can make a name for yourself, violates its sovereign dignity. It can't *correct* you when you put words in its mouth. So, yes, as an ethnographer I fucking disagree with the entire premise."

Sufficiently eviscerated, Sean pushed her chair from the table and crossed her arms over her stomach. "What's your solution, then, do nothing? Resign and sit around petting the dog, moping about the end of the world?"

"God, Sean, you are so astoundingly, myopically self-centered it shocks me. I don't know if it's getting worse or if I ignored it before." Riya stared at her, a deep maroon flush blooming across her brown cheeks. "I'm tired of listening to you talk about *what this'll do for you* without an ounce of ethical consideration. You're grabbing for cash that could be spent on pragmatic interventions for actual habitat stabilization, or assisting with disaster refugee displacement, or whatever else, but those projects aren't as sexy. It's all appearances with you. This grant could fund my department's grad researchers, who I will remind you are almost *all* working with peoples and places whose experiences of climate catastrophe are on the knife's edge, several times over. And why are wolves your focal point, anyway? Why not rats, they're better survivors. Because people think wolves are cool."

"You're not from here. The wolves surviving means something about us surviving," Sean said, then bit her tongue immediately at the startled grimace that washed over Riya's face. *Not from here.* "Wait, I didn't mean it like that—"

"Wow, no, you're done talking," Riya said.

Without another word she picked up her bowl in one hand, her plate in the other, and left the kitchen to sit on the couch. Miller trotted after. Visible through the wide-mouthed entrance to the other room, her squared shoulders radiated anger. Sean sipped her water, embarrassed. That fight hadn't felt the same as the last six or seven— or ten. The debate beginning with her research dove through to a nastier set of problems underneath. *It's all about appearances with you* stung in her chest. After Riya failed to return to the table for another half hour, Sean slunk to the fridge to store her leftovers and retreated behind the closed door of the office.

Four weeks later, the grant was approved to ample fanfare in the pop-science press: *neuroscientists to study how iconic remaining wild wolves think, ushering in a promising era of connection between human and nonhuman animals.* The head of the committee who'd denied her internal funding sent a congratulatory email, which she cracked a fresh bottle of scotch to gloat over. The savor of victory soured a fraction when Riya refused to come to the department celebration on her arm, citing unfinished grading. Sean found a therapist's business card on her desk the following morning with a short note reading, *make an appointment.*

Over four monitors spread throughout the lab, the team watched Dr. June and her assistant return Kate to the forest via ATV, secured across the safe-rack like a huge swaddled child. The trap-camera captured one angle and the assistant's cell phone another. At the tree line, the pair of them hustled the wolf's ungainly body to the ground. The assistant unwrapped the animal and swept her from tail to snout with the camera. The patch-film Dr. June had applied was roughly the same shade as Kate's skin below her coat, hiding her stitches.

"She'll be alert in fifteen to twenty minutes," June said to the microphone. "We'll wait with the ATV until she starts to come 'round, then we'll book it. The pack should approach her soon."

Sean sipped a cold brew, monitoring the unconscious wolf and her team at turns. Alex and Dahye paced the length of the dimmed lab windows in muted conversation with one another, Christian idled at the coffee maker waiting for their fourth refill, Aseem spun his studio chair at precise 180-degree turns with a kick of each heel, left-right-left-right. Two research assistants, one technician for the interface, a fellow neuroscientist, and herself, the researcher-subject.

A commotion startled them all as the ATV revved and Dr. June announced, "There she goes!"

Kate's left hindquarter flexed, paw scrabbling at the earth. Her ears flicked and her jaw muscles tensed. As engine roar filled the lab, the RA's prurient camera zoomed in on her half-alert face, tongue working across a row of yellowed teeth while one eyelid fluttered. Aseem stopped spinning. Sean held her breath. If they'd damaged her . . .

Kate lifted her head on an unsteady neck and growled.

"Go," June barked to her RA.

The assistant passed her the camera and drove them away while Kate receded from view. Her legs wobbled under her as she stood, sat, stood again. The trap-camera broadcasted her stagger into the woods, loopy from sedation but promisingly mobile. Sean sighed deep in her gut. The chip tracker showed Kate moving farther into the forest; matching blips for the remainder of the pack ranged a few miles out, nearer the creek than the field-line.

"What if it doesn't work?" Aseem groaned, echoing Sean's own worries.

"We're about to find out," Christian responded. "Ready for setup, boss?"

Sean drained the last milky gulp of her coffee and thumped the mason jar onto the table. On-screen, Dr. June and the RA began breaking down their field surgery site. In an hour there would be no record of their presence aside from the ruts in the field, the neural mesh in the wolf's skull, and the data Sean intended to broadcast into her own. And if she failed, there might as well be nothing at all—just her wife's *I told you so* and her public career crash.

"Let's do this thing," she said.

At the south end of the lab, Dahye unlocked the interfacing room first with the physical key and then with the digital access code. Alex bounded into the room with his sterile prep kit to wipe down the "magic machine," as June had referred to it. Aseem tapped away on the lab's main computer, shifting camera feeds to program feeds, research notes, and the interface's readout. Its cursor blinked eagerly on an otherwise blank screen. Christian stood beside Sean's chair, silent for a beat, as her fingertips tapped nervously on the armrest.

Steadying, they asked, "Are you comfortable with the procedures, Dr. Kell-Luddon?"

"I remember them," Sean said.

She thought her skin would vibrate off her bones if she had to wait for much longer, pretending to be calm. All the sacrifice and uncertainty of the past twenty-six months had led to this moment; her team bustled through their first execution of protocols, turning like a well-oiled gear. But what use was a performance of competence if the results fell through? People remembered failures longer than successes. Sean steadied her breathing, five-counts in through her nose and out through her mouth.

"I think we're good to go," Christian said as Alex gave them the thumbs-up.

Sean followed them into the hospital-bare cubby containing the machine's interface: a giant padded recliner resembling an upscale dentist's chair with gnarled limbs of cables sprouting from its head-rest, arms, and frame. The helmet looked like a salon blow-dryer—the gentle padded restraints for the subject's limbs, not so much, unless it was a *very* particular kind of salon. Christian wheeled their tool cart to the desk in the far corner and gestured for Sean to settle in. As they wiped her scarred temple with a sterile pad, astringent scent invading her nostrils, their pale gray eyes flicked to meet hers.

"We'll activate when the map shows her approaching the pack," Sean said.

"Aye-aye," Christian agreed.

The plush recliner sucked her into its embrace. Though the prep was painless, Sean's physical reaction to being strapped in belied her discomfort—racing pulse, cold prickling washes of nerves. Christian's hands were sure on the restraints, firm on her wrists and ankles. Their brow furrowed with concentration as they adjusted the neck brace and lined up the edges of the helmet before lowering it and locking the mechanism into place. The visor screen was blank, sensory deprivation plunging Sean abruptly into nothingness. No sound, no sight, nothing outside of her thrumming flesh and blood. The fact that the Chilson-Reed interface had originally been designed for treating post-traumatic stress and degenerative memory disorders made her darkly, briefly chuckle. Aside from the wildly prohibitive costs to the uninsured, Sean had a feeling being trapped in a sensory void while a machine reprogrammed your brain's chemical functions might be traumatic enough on its own. The three trial runs she'd gone through to test her own uplink hadn't been pleasant.

Through the helmet's speakers, Christian said: "Comfortable and secure?"

Sean gave a sideways thumbs-up. Leather stuck to her stress-wet palms.

"Your readouts are coming through normal, though elevated general arousal, obviously. Reception is at standby-active, you're in the machine," they confirmed. "I'll give you a countdown once Kate starts to approach. Her transmission is broadcast-active too, FYI, but until we flip the proverbial switch your interface won't import it. No errors so far."

Only in the emptiness could Sean, edgy and nauseous, admit to herself, *I'm about to pipe another brain into my brain.* She would become the researcher-subject, the every(wo)man scientist hero, unless the first attempt scrambled her gray matter bad enough to sink the whole project. Animal trials had gone fine, humans using the original program were fine, safety protocols were in place. And yet, she was abruptly terrified. Riya had given her a perfunctory kiss on the cheek over a pot of grits that morning, and Sean hadn't told her it was launch-day; she hadn't said, *hey, I love you, in case I die or something.* Too focused on preparing herself for the big event.

"Approaching," Christian announced crisply. "Five, four, three, two—"

One faded into a tinny hum as the linkage queued. The stench of alcohol swab disappeared beneath a rich wash of olfactory input, smell so intense it held texture inside her skull. Visuals swam across the projection screen in saturated colors, initially blinding. After a moment they established a readable pattern before her eyes, as if the creek bed were running through a series of photo filters. The interface programming struggled to render a human-accessible spectrum from the more-than-human input pouring from the wolf's neural system. Sean's nose, or more accurately her cognitive processes for scent, overloaded with stinking data: *loam-dirt-piss-trees-family-home.* Last came the jolting impact of four legs loping, a powerful haunch and spread paws with claws grabbing earth; restraints dug into human skin and bone with tender security as she instinctually attempted to match the sense of movement with reality. Sean wrestled for clarity through the phantom sensorium, dug for herself beneath her sublimation within another being. Protocol for processing disorientation or overload was to repeat her name and address and the date; her flexible human lips and tongue moved across dull slick teeth as she began to mutter, "Sean Kull-Luddon, 279 Rogers Parkway—"

A yipping howl bloomed from her left, its frantic edge calling her home so firmly that she—Sean, or the wolf—spurred into a sprint despite her sore head and unwieldy muscles. Once again the chemical saturation bowled over Sean's distancing protocols, rolling her consciousness under the relief of barreling into her sibling's body at full speed. The wolves rolled across the loamy forest floor, slobbering on faces and chewing ears and outpouring *love*. The startling recognition of a specific feeling—plus the cracking stretch of her own heaving rib cage—offered Sean a brief psychic harbor to cast anchor in; she hitched herself onto an immediate drive to name the wolf's desire, to tie her own desire neatly around it. *Think, don't just feel.* Translating through speech and language, Sean split her attentions between the staggering wealth of affective input and her critical understanding of those inputs; she catalogued Kate's relief at seeing her sibling again, after such a frightful happening, and she breathed easier. The wolf had a whole and particular grammar of knowing and naming. When the remainder of the pack arrived moments later, Sean had no need for the names her team had given them any longer—the scents differentiated them, scents she couldn't cross-reference while swimming through the midst of so much soupy qualia.

The shutoff triggered and the data flood cut, abrupt.

Sean smashed against the loss like a concrete wall, her sudden self-isolation triggering a savage, throbbing headache. She pried her clenched jaw apart and worked saliva across her dry teeth while the muscles at the front of her throat spasmed from overuse. Already, the intensity of feeling had begun to wash loose—except for the alien, beautiful ease with which the wolf had fallen back into her family. When Christian eased the helmet off, Sean grunted through a snotty nose, "Holy fuck."

Stuffed into a corner booth at an off-campus bar, Sean and her team radiated exhausted, punchy glee. Their bored young waiter dispensed pint glasses all around, plus one brown-bottled craft soda for Alex. Dahye's box-square grin had become a steady fixture after the third and final interface activation—the first attempt where Sean maintained her internal balance instead of drowning in the influx. She'd done a burst of hasty journaling once the machine spat her out that last time, scribbling all of the events she'd piggybacked on plus the emotions and instincts and *real fucking thoughts* of the wolf. Discounting the vibrant pain lodged behind her orbital bones, Sean was riding higher than god. Thanks to Christian's long preparatory labors with Aseem, the interface's nonstop recordings of impulses, signals, responses, and so on had flawlessly siphoned loads of data while the fantastical electric meat of Sean's body and brain translated it in real time. Even after the human portion of the observations ended, that raw data could serve as a treasure trove.

Dahye lifted her pint and said, "To us, for making history."

"To all of you, more than me," Sean corrected—though on the inside, she classified all of their actions under the possessive umbrella of her labor and direction.

Her team; her results; her lab; her wolf.

The rims of glasses clinked with frantic energy. Sean swallowed a fizzy, sweet mouthful of the most expensive option on draft—a pear cider—and let a long exhale seep from her belly. What did it mean, to make history? The accomplishment blipped on her radar for a moment before the mountain of work that remained rose overhead. At the front of the pub, the double doors swung open with a gust of chill air. Riya stood framed in evening lamplight, a jaunty mustard scarf draped across her throat and the right shoulder of her leather jacket. Hands in her pockets, she scanned the room, catching Sean dumbstruck at the figure she cut.

And then, she smiled. Cool red lipstick, a handsome flash of teeth, threads of silver shining in the thick waves of her black hair; the golden tinge of the pub lighting made her dark skin glow. Since the grant celebration, neither of them had appeared at one of the other's work-related gatherings. Sean had to admit, her reception among colleagues had gone stiff without Riya's steady assistance. A détente appeared to have begun, though Sean couldn't guess why tonight was the night. She swallowed another mouthful of cider to

ease her parched throat while her wife approached the table, unzip-
ping her jacket over a cream shell blouse tucked into high-waisted
black jeans. Dahye whistled approvingly and Riya winked in response as she took her seat beside Sean.

"I hear the first trial was a success, huh," she said.

Sean handed over her cider without being asked. Riya took a sip
while the team talked over one another with the percussive gush of a
tapped keg: Alex's "should have seen it," Dahye's "so cool," Aseem's
"we're pleased," and Christian's "no errors." Riya laughed her performance laugh, the one that rolled out handsomely baritone. Sean
laid a hand on her thigh. It was the same charismatic laugh that
had caught her dead to rights across a room at a speaker's reception
bringing together several departments, nine years earlier.

"I'm glad your work paid off," she murmured, covering Sean's
hand for a squeeze.

"Kate is the real reason we're here," Sean said. Riya's concern for
the animal lay self-consciously on her mind. The smelly panting
breath of packmates haunted the root of her own tongue, a remnant
of the cognitive enormity of sharing in the wolf's self. "So maybe a
toast for her sake, as our window into another world. She'll be our
North Star."

"And to Chilson-Reed, for that fat stack of cash," Riya snarked,
but she lifted the cider regardless.

Christian snorted. "Cheers to that!"

Sean wove her fingers across Riya's on the glass. The sight of their
hands laid double, ashy-knuckled white and wind-chapped brown
with matching platinum bands on the wedding fingers, soothed a
fearful knot in Sean's gut. From the outside nothing was amiss: the
image of their marriage maintained its progressive gloss, the role-
model faculty couple students could gush about over brunch. *Life-
goals, wife-goals.* Glasses clinked again. Individual conversations
kicked up, the team splitting into pairs and trios, while Riya and
Sean sat in a bubble of quiet at their edge of the booth.

"Thank you for coming out," Sean said finally.

"Of course I did, what else should a partner expect?" Riya replied
with a sticky sweet peck on the cheek. Sean heard the message underneath loud and clear.

6 months prior

Therapist waiting rooms were the dullest possible liminal spaces. Sean chewed her fat boba tea straw between her molars, the inside of her mouth syrup-filmed. Riya had introduced her to the stuff on date four and she'd never gone back. The television played reruns of a real estate show. Its protagonists were a middle-management couple fleeing rising sea levels in the Keys, due to consume their entire neighborhood within the next two to five years. Their budget was a modest $900,000. Plastic stabbed Sean's gums as she gnawed. One downside of shifting to midafternoon appointments: the people before her had a chance to go long. Jonas had racked up a fifteen-minute delay.

Finally, the door swung open and his smiling face appeared, white hair slicked back and mustache neat. Sean followed him down the hall, past a static noise machine and closed doors, into an office with a plush green couch, mahogany coffee table, and brown leather chair. She took her usual seat, stacked a pillow under her right arm, and set her unfinished drink aside.

"How're you this week?" Jonas asked.

"I scheduled the surgical date with Chilson-Reed. It's next month," she said. Not that she expected otherwise, but his expression remained neutral as he gestured her onward. "I haven't told Riya that I agreed to, uh, be the subject."

"Wasn't it a toss-up between you and Dr. Shukla?" Jonas asked.

Sean propped her chin on one hand and replied, "Honestly, no, it was always going to be me. I'm the one who spearheaded the project, I want to be the one who does it. I'd prefer to be the one going on NPR later, you know?"

"So why haven't you told your partner yet?" Jonas asked.

"I guess because she doesn't approve? You know we've been fighting about it since before I even got the grant. Since I started outlining it."

"It seems you've set yourself a time limit for telling her, if surgery's scheduled so soon," he said.

Sean glanced out the window, five stories up from a parking lot with a Starbucks on the other end. Cars flashed past on the freeway beyond a distant retaining wall. *I don't have to tell her,* sprang to mind, but she discarded the thought as both functionally impossible and also probably the reason she had to go to therapy to begin with. Lack of communication, emotional distance, failure to reciprocate the labor of marriage; or as Riya had summed up the issue after Sean didn't show to yet another anthropology outing, *catastrophic selfishness*.

"I don't want to," she admitted.

"Why not?" he asked.

"Because I don't want the extra stress of arguing about my project's ethics again, when we're never going to agree," she said.

"I'm not sure that's the whole reason. We've also been discussing your expectations for the marriage, and hers, through the lens of these professional arguments—in particular, problems with work-life balance and reciprocally supporting her career as much as she does yours. You said you were willing to put in more effort, but have you told her that? Or made concrete plans for how you'll do so?"

Jonas sipped from his lavender coffee mug with one ankle crossed over the opposite knee. Facing judgement-free but nonetheless unpleasant prompting, Sean caved in an instant. His patrician, comforting persona peeled her defenses as efficiently as a ripe banana; being petulant or resistant made her feel immature, and that rankled her worse than being honest.

"Fuck, of course I haven't." She sighed.

She never took his good, pragmatic advice to improve her relationship or herself. On some level, she was amazed he hadn't given her a referral after so little progress. Another sip of tea with three sticky boba to chew filled her mouth for a long pause. Jonas would, as she well knew, allow the silence to settle as long as she did.

So she continued, "She doesn't understand the reason I need to be the one who uses the interface. I've dreamed about this since I was a kid, you know? But she's not supporting me, or even letting me *have* it. She thinks it's selfish, but the world is fucking ending all around us, and the wolves are probably going to be gone in our lifetime, so I just want to . . . *connect*. Seriously, that's it."

"If you want so badly to connect," Jonas began, tapping his fingers on the edge of his mug. Sean let her gaze skate over his and out the window again. "Then perhaps talking openly to your partner, the woman you married, would be a better place to start. You're chasing another creature to give you the intimacy you're craving, a being that can't reciprocate your desire the way Riya can and has. There's also, as I know you're aware, an unavoidable racialized and gendered dynamic to the inequities she's expressing her concerns over."

"Goddamn, Jonas," punched out of her mouth without her consent.

"I'd like you to sit with that thought, work through what your approaches might be to seeing her perspective. We can change the topic, for now," he offered, but the assessment had already burrowed through her ear canals to lodge in her hindbrain. "Are you planning to avoid the conversation until closer to the surgical date?"

She groaned. "No, I need to tell her. Let's brainstorm how the hell I do that."

Two weeks into the project, the wolf pack brought down a skinny doe before the lab crew got up and running. Out of sheer dumb luck, the kill occurred in range of a camera. Sean stood watching a replay of the footage, observing the wolves—whose identities she recalled through their scents as much as their given names at this point— perform the cooperative ritual of a meal. The lead pair, aged into the danger zone for wild wolves, first devoured steaming viscera and flesh, then the adolescent nudged in for his fill, and finally Kate and the rest of the familial group gnawed until nothing remained but grizzled fur and bones. Sean, nibbling a salad with sliced tempeh on top, felt chest-loosening *relief* at the sight of the carnage: today it was feast, not famine.

"Ready, boss?" Christian called across the room.

"As ever," she said, setting her unfinished lunch on the worktop.

During the first week Sean couldn't stop wondering if Chilson-Reed had outsourced their padded restraints to a hospital manu-facturer or a bondage retailer, but she'd since become inured to the weirdest parts of the prep. Wrists and ankles secured, head locked in a black box, long minutes of utter deprivation; she'd started to look forward to the process. Trackers showed the heavy-bellied pack in a settled cluster. While Sean had ridden along for hundreds of miles of loping, forest-spanning hunts, there had been no good opportunities to observe freshly sated rest. Christian read the countdown as Sean caught her breath, eager heart thumping at her ribs.

Data blossomed across the machine projection and the inside of her nerves simultaneously, lighting up her receptors as she swam through the initial disorienting burst. Regular usage had smoothed out the worst kinks, which she avoided considering too hard, given those kinks were located within the matter of her brain. The instant the link established Sean twitched in the seat, unsure of the scrambled wash of colors and impressions dumped onto her—

—which cleared into grogginess as Kate unfurled from her tail-over-nose circle, arising from a nap. Sean breathed shallowly as she relocated her separate consciousness, the world resolving into flattened Technicolor. Had Kate been *dreaming* when the interface activated? Had that connection somehow nudged her mind to waking? Should be impossible, within the presumptive mono-directionality of the feed. Sean got inside Kate; Kate didn't get inside Sean. She wriggled her human pelvis in the recliner while Kate stretched her own hips, setting her consternation aside to sink under the surface of their communion. Easier with practice, Sean slid out of her language-oriented processing to the meditative role of phantom-inside-alien-flesh. Dispersing herself without losing herself, like a solution of oil and vinegar, fatty and stinging on the tongue. Words were for after the feed cut her loose from the rush of *being* something else.

The adolescent with the pure white snout yipped at the center of the familial pile. She groaned an invitation while lolling onto her side with legs outstretched, stuffed to the brim and jaw-sore. Blood lingered around her gums, the temporary funk of security. He stomped and clambered over resisting bodies and groggily nipping teeth, runtish though approaching his second year. His snout dug into her neck as he pushed their cheeks together. The smell of him was hale and whole, healthy enough. She caught his ear for a gentle bite, fur tickling the roof of her mouth. Sensations shaped like *affection* and *worry* and *protect* coasted through Sean's head. Full bellies and the gentle, glowing warmth of sun filtered through trees. The pup's big paws, which he'd grow into if he survived another winter, caused a welcome silly pain as he clambered all over her, attempting to wrestle. She kicked him once. *Indulgent.*

Lingering underneath: fear and privation, the knowledge of ice, small cold bodies.

Her connection to the interface ceased. Sean heaved a centering breath; she curled her toes and ground her dull teeth into her pale lips to remind herself of her real shape. Christian unhooked the restraints from her wrists and ankles while the silent black box around her head gave her the space to settle all the pinging chemicals and impulses. Her notebooks for recording immediate recollections waited in the main lab; the interface and its behemoth databanks recorded the raw material. But as Christian's thumbs brushed her collarbone while releasing her skull from the machine's maw, translating those intimate moments through the lens of her knowledge of what would likely come next—in a few days, a few weeks—seemed too grim to bear.

"You all right?" Christian asked as they lifted the helmet free.

Sean had no siblings, least of all a younger brother. Observation protocol suggested she maintain a healthy distance, but by nature of the research, she had no distance from her object—subject?—of study. The wolf lingered, a phantom self. Her journals had become the place she recorded all her stories of affect, of impossible closeness, of *emotion*. None of that language would be acceptable for a peer-reviewed scientific publication, though, and the drafts she typed up for the cloud drive leaned toward the cleanly clinical. What language could communicate the *longing for a future* she'd felt without stooping to anthropomorphizing—or, without giving the appearance of having done so to a derisive colleague? Bringing standpoint into an otherwise quantitative project was one thing, but it was another to be too free with her emotions in her data.

Eventually, through a sandy mouth, Sean said, "Yeah, I'm fine."

She chafed her upper arms warm, eyes squinting against the searing sun pouring into the main lab from its overlook windows. Coming back to the sterile brightness after an intense session—surrounded by other people who'd expect her to speak calmly and concisely—presented a challenge. "Sean" wafted through the air, a loose tuft of fur on the wind, her cognition scrambled and uneasy. Aseem and Dahye were bent heads-together over the readouts on one screen, bickering about some tiny detail. Sean's unfinished salad sat waiting for her. With great mechanical effort, she crossed the room and picked it up, gazing into the wilted leafy depths.

"Can't believe how long this fall is holding out," Alex said from his desk. "We need the weather to break if we're aiming for solid data on their cooperative behaviors. We need some survival-based necessities to crop up."

Sean stared at him. He raised a curious eyebrow, light caught in the auburn threading of his unshaved scruff. His plain face, the same face Sean had seen five days of the week for several years, appeared suddenly strange to her. She swallowed a mouthful of sick-spit and dumped her salad in the trash can.

II

A t 10 a.m., the air was crisp and the breeze nippy. Sean jostled her messenger bag strap, sloshing an open mug of coffee from home while trekking across the research campus. People bustled from building to building, walking irreverently across the green lawn. She'd luxuriously slept in, and awoken to find Riya gone for her Tuesday seminar. Chasing an instinctive urge she'd buried her face in Riya's pillow and huffed ripe lungfuls of sleepsweat, old drool, and a wispy haunt of perfume. No one was home to see her, and she figured she'd earned at least one delayed arrival to the lab, so instead of rising from bed she clamped the pillowcase between her teeth—gnawing the fabric damp as she humped out a lazy, effusive orgasm on the other pillow, the one Riya squeezed between her knees and thighs while she slept.

She felt closer to her wife's absent warmth, surrounded in scent and softness, and considered sending her a surprise photograph. Given the state of their relationship, though, an unprompted nude seemed presumptuous. Nevertheless, as she left the house the aliveness of her body struck her: a giddy afterglow of tingling naughtiness at spending the morning jerking off when she should've been heading for the office.

As the backside of her building arose in the distance, her phone buzzed in her front jeans pocket. Multiple pulses, a call rather than a text; she juggled her bag-strap-plus-coffee to retrieve it. The display read *Alex Trib*.

Paused standing on the quad, she answered, "Hey, I'm almost there."

"Uh, maybe turn around," Alex said tightly.

"What?"

"Apparently, we've got protestors," he replied.

Sean squinted across the lawn but saw nothing of the sort. "Out front, I guess?"

"Security has the building on lockdown and is trying to get them to disperse. But you definitely can't get in through the crowd, and they seem a little rowdy, so . . ." He trailed off.

"Why are they protesting us?" she asked, bewildered.

"Judging from the signage . . ." He paused. Other voices chattered in the background with muffled agitation. "Animal cruelty, conservation not exploitation, and stuff in that general vein."

Irritation shredded through her afterglow. "Are you kidding me? Don't they have actual exploitation to scream about, instead of harassing someone trying to help?"

"Yeah, I suspect our definitions of *help* might be kinda different."

Sean set off again, boots forcefully thumping pavement. Alex was quiet on the other end of the line. She took the opposite of her usual route, approaching from the flanking side for a glimpse.

"You're still coming, aren't you?" Alex grumbled.

"Yep," she said.

She couldn't quite jog with the sloshing coffee, but she tried her best. On the other end of the line, Alex announced something to the team. Sean paused on the sidewalk to absorb the fracas from a safe distance: four campus security officers, whom she was theoretically not a fan of, talking to a cluster of fifteen or twenty people with signs. Sean had done her time in climate protests and Pride marches; she wasn't a total sellout, her wife's criticisms aside, but a randy, aggravated part of her wanted to shout that this was her turf—that she was doing the research to understand the animals they claimed to represent. She wasn't doing Kate harm, and the accusation that she didn't feel for and alongside her was a raw insult. For that matter, the wolf had no awareness of being observed, nor the fact that Sean existed. Otherwise, the whole project would've been moot.

Her phone buzzed an incoming text directly against her ear. Chaos erupted on the other end of the line. She distinctly heard Dahye yelp, "Oh, shit!"

Sean held her phone in front of her face to read the campus alert:

Please evacuate Health Research Buildings 2 and 4, per credible threat, in an orderly . . .

Her heart leapt into her throat as she stared at the big glass-fronted building a few hundred feet from her. The building containing her team, her interface, and her research notes. A policeman's walkie-talkie crackled loudly, proclaiming a code something-or-other. Sean stood paralyzed, frozen between flight and the urge to do something, anything. A splash of hot coffee across her wrist, soaking into her sleeve, provided a physical jolt. Her hands were shaking.

"Get out of there, I'll meet you at the president's office," she said to Alex, who was hollering directions to the team, before she hung up.

After two long hours of conversation with security and public relations, Sean led her team to the nearest café for a caffeine boost paid for with her personal card, gave them each a stiff hug, and sent them home for their mandated three days off. An impotent anger twisted in her guts. According to the security staff, the protesters had nothing to do with the threat—*probably fake but can't be too sure*—which didn't surprise her. She'd said something to the effect of, "I'm not an asshole, let them yell at us if they want, just . . . maybe in a more organized, less disruptive fashion." That made her feel like a genuine asshole. How the mighty had fallen, onto the side of the man.

According to the protest organizer, the reason for the sudden attention was an interview with a Chilson-Reed talking head in the digital edition of *Popular Science* about the project they'd bankrolled—with no warnings, fact-checking, or corrections requested from the project team. Ensconced on the couch at home, her legs tucked underneath her with a twinge in the right kneecap, Sean propped her laptop on her thigh to scroll for the offending post. She had to admit, she was just as miffed about the interview being blog fodder as she was about the lack of consultation; their project deserved more fanfare. Miller, curled on the cushion next to her, tried to lay his head over the keyboard as she read:

The Future of Biotech:
Human and Animal Minds Converge!

November 3, 2031 4:35 p.m.

On behalf of all the readers who've ever wondered what it's like to be a wolf, we sat down with Marketing VP Craig Henderson of Chilson-Reed Pharmaceuticals and Biotechnologies to discuss the project their company is funding over the next eighteen months: research into the minds of animals via their state-of-the-art neurological interface. Throughout human history until now, our observation of animals has been limited to watching their behaviors, guessing about their motivations, and anthropomorphizing our pets. With the C. R. interface, originally designed for psychiatric use, researchers are able to peek into the feelings and thoughts of an individual animal—like Kate, the gray wolf whose interior life is being experienced and recorded by a dedicated team at the University of Minnesota.

"I believe this project opens us up to a whole world of virtual reality experiences," Henderson said, when asked about the potential applications of the research. "If the technology can be put to use in more than clinical applications, particularly if the production cost and challenge of implantation goes down for the casual American user, then in a few years we could all subscribe to feeds of our favorite animals—like watching livestreams of wolf packs, but you'd really feel what they're going through!"

Though the project has only been running for approximately three weeks, the data Chilson-Reed has received has them excited about commercial applications and further development of their technological outreach frameworks. Using a neural mesh implanted in the subject animal, the C. R. interface ports chemical and sensory data to the human user, mapping the animal's mind as closely as possible onto the user's. Henderson continued, "The experience of being a wolf is so unique, and has so much to show us about ourselves and how we

Sean smacked her laptop closed. Commercial applications her ass. That wasn't in the terms of the grant, nor the intellectual property rights reserved, nor the proposal for conservation applications of the data on project completion. And who the fuck was Craig Henderson? Craig Henderson, in *marketing*? Selling her transcendental experiences as a video game wasn't why she stuck a transmitter into her gray matter, or their wolf's. No wonder people decided to stage a protest. Six livid emails later—including one CC to the team to make them aware of the context, one to the CEO of Chilson-Reed, and another to their investments director—Sean cracked her aching hands.

Aseem's text appeared on her phone as she was washing a pound of summer squash, zucchini, and eggplant: *Are you really surprised? Corporate is as corporate does, it's not fed funding.* Sean ground her teeth, flung water off her hands, and set to making ratatouille. That was what Riya had written on the fridge planner for the night's dinner. Her version probably wouldn't taste as good, but she desperately needed to do something with her hands—and for once she was home first. As she stood rough-chopping vegetables alone, were Kate and the pup, their sisters and brothers and parents, all nestled in a smelly companionable pile without her? The suburban solitude roused an itchy, marrow-deep loneliness that nothing in her life had been able to fill.

Ratatouille bubbled on the stove, scenting the kitchen with tomato and garlic. Sean sat cross-legged on the floor scratching Miller's belly. His tail thumped like an offbeat metronome on the tile, counting two-four then three-eight. She cooed at him for his rank, nasty doggy-breath. She'd give him a dental treat after she got up to finish cooking. Warm fur and a wriggly body under her grooming hands were more important than bad breath. Until the front door opened, forty-five minutes before Sean expected Riya home.

"Sean, are you home?" Riya called out.

"In the kitchen," she hollered back.

Heels clacked across the hardwood—rare, leaving her shoes on—and Riya paused on the threshold of the kitchen. Her drawn brows pinched wrinkles onto her forehead. Her glance flicked from the Dutch oven on the stovetop, to wife and dog on the floor, to the pre-set dinner table.

"Why didn't you tell me you were evacuated for a *bomb threat*?" she asked, leaping straight over the domestic tableaux.

Miller pawed at Sean's frozen hands. She resumed lackluster, distracted petting as she gazed up at Riya. Her lack of response yawned between them, a chasm. She fumbled, "I didn't think it was a big deal, I wasn't sure you'd—"

"Did you think I wouldn't care?" Riya asked.

Hurt bubbled under a quaver in Riya's voice, the lilt of her question wincing. She collapsed into a seat at the table; her gaze bounced from

Sean's silent thin-lipped mouth back to the sink full of prep-dishes. Miller's toenails scraped Sean's forearm as he pawed again, demanding her continued attention, but she shushed him and scooted on her butt to settle next to Riya's chair. Her wife breathed shallowly, a hand covering her mouth, as if by force of will she might stop herself from crying.

"I'm sorry," Sean said. "Security told us it wasn't serious, so I just came home and started cooking. I haven't done that in a while. And I've been trying to keep the project out of the house, you know, because we fight about it so much, so—"

Riya cut in, "I want to be grateful to come home to you making dinner, but I was so worried. Karen asked me how you were holding up, and I didn't even know what she was talking about. What if the threat had been serious?"

"You usually don't check your phone at work," Sean deflected.

"But when I did check, I had a university alert and nothing from my wife. I had to lie and say you'd texted me that it was all right," she said.

Sean sighed through her nose. Wrecking the afternoon hadn't been her intention. She drew one of Riya's lusciously expensive boots heel-first onto her thigh. Silver-white stitches crossing the black leather matched the silver buckled straps at the ankle. One hand steadying her muscled calf and the other wrapped around the short heel, Sean eased her boot free and set it carefully aside. Her fingertips glided over the silky, day-wear damp sock, then unrolled it from cuff downward. Riya's toes flexed once she'd bared them to the air, their matching blue polish on the nails slightly chipped. How long had it been since she'd done Riya this small service? Sean removed the other boot and sock with equal care, then dug her thumbs into the arch of Riya's foot. She anticipated a groan of pleasure but instead received a sigh.

Riya said, "What happened to us, Sean? Even when you're here, I'm lonely. You don't really see me. Sometimes I feel like you're making a checklist of things you imagine a 'good scholar husband' should do for her housewife, instead of listening to what I, your colleague and companion and *equal*, am asking you for. And—I can't just keep living with it."

Sean swallowed, Riya's words sinking from the crown of her head

to the bowl of her hips like a cold stone. She glanced up with trep-
idation. The expression she found on her wife's face was desolate,
tired. Her massaging hands had stilled, but releasing the foot she
held firm between them seemed both impossibly awkward and impossibly terrible. When, precisely, had she gone wrong after the easy
comradery of their courtship—or, their first few years of marriage?
She had been so enamored by Riya's wit and style, her astounding competence. Her own overtures, when she'd offered them, had
made Riya liquid with desire. For a moment, she wished Riya was
as impressed with her as she used to be, despite the hollows beneath
her glossy surface myriad failures had revealed.

"I do love you, though. So much," Sean said.

"I know. But abstract love isn't the problem. Shit like this afternoon is the problem," Riya said.

Her ankle shifted, as if she intended to stand; Sean instead resumed
her massage with a long, full-palmed stroke. She used both thumbs to
trace either side of Riya's ankle tendon, and her toes squeezed in reflex. What could Sean give of herself? Maybe, an ounce of the truth.

"When I left for home, I was angry. I wasn't thinking about
much aside from that." After another moment, she continued, "*Pop
Sci* published some dumb puff piece from Chilson-Reed that makes
us sound like we're running a circus experiment. That drew the protesters. I just didn't want to argue about it again with you too."

Riya's leg tensed a miniscule fraction.

"I wouldn't . . . resent this project as much if it didn't feel as if it
represented our bigger issues, you know." She lifted her foot from
Sean's grip and planted it on her shoulder, arch settling across her
trapezius muscle. Sean tilted her head to kiss her calf, from habit as
much as want. *We're working on it,* she thought. Then Riya continued, softer, "But seeing how you treat your team, and the wolf pack,
and the research itself makes me aware that—maybe, I'm on the
same tier. I'm an object; you consume me, use me to build yourself
up, put me in your story. Do you even know what course I'm teach-
ing this term, or what I'm revising when I'm at the office? Do you
read my work anymore?"

Tired of being left out, and with the impeccable timing of all
dogs sensing a disturbance, Miller burrowed his snout into Sean's
armpit from behind. She yelped, ticklish, and Riya's foot slid off of

her shoulder; the oven timer dinged. Fragile détente shattered, Riya stood and retrieved her discarded boots. Sean stayed seated on the floor, scruffing Miller, absorbing the anguish on her wife's round, sweet face.

"Sometimes I'm not sure you see anyone besides yourself as a person," she said.

The knife struck home. Sean ducked her head with a cringe as her wife left the room—shoulders slumped by the cruelty of telling the unvarnished truth. The timer dinged again. Sean got up to turn the stove off, and neither of them returned to the argument over a quiet, strained dinner.

Wrapped in a robe and slippers against the cutting wind starting to blow down from the north the following morning, Sean carried her coffee and a notepad onto the back deck. Imagining the wolves in their warm huddle, sleeping while the season faltered around them, made her belly seize briefly. Knowing how much Kate *understood* winter's approach and her family's weaknesses—her clear, emotionally articulate conceptions of threat and loss—weighed on Sean's conscience. To bury that haunting problem underneath a more immediate issue, she'd sketched out a to-do list cribbed from the dusty chore board. Mopping the downstairs, washing the baseboards, getting Miller groomed, reorganizing the pots-and-pans drawer. Economic security being what it was, each floor of the house had a dedicated vacuum robot, but their capabilities were limited.

The night before, lying awake and listening to Riya snore, she weighed the prospect that her marriage had gone from cooling to failing. Wasn't it enough at their stage of life to be decently matched in their careers and able to function within one another's orbits? Fissures she'd been able to smooth over before spread into chasms—as if once Riya peered into her rotten emptied core, past the veneers of competence and charm and concern, those hollow parts were all she could see. And she had a point that sending her a check-in text hadn't crossed Sean's mind; even she could see how fucked up that was.

Their life together was crumbling, slipping through her grasp.

She spent the day rotating between apologetic emails from Chilson-Reed, texts to her team about small tasks that could be done from home VPNs, and her list of unfinished housework. Riya returned from campus to a far cleaner home than she left. It had been a long time since anyone cleaned those baseboards, in what Sean realized might have been a one-sided stalemate over her failure to pull her weight. In turn, Riya kissed her like a trophy, ate the dinner she'd prepared, then ate *her* for dessert, which was increasingly rare. Underneath the almost-filmic domestic evening lingered a bad taste, though, a gloss of unreality—as if the pair of them were each acting the life they'd rather be living, for the sake of a minute's respite. Sean slept fitfully, dreaming of tails tickling noses, baying howls in the dark, and shrunken hungry bellies.

On her second day away from the lab, she tried to pass her time similarly, but loneliness increased its thorny itch. Fighting a strange skin hunger, Sean ended up spending two hours awkwardly pillowed beside Miller on his dog bed. Riya came home late, citing student meetings, and slipped off to bed early. Sean accidentally drifted to sleep on the couch, only to startle from a nightmare about cracked toenails and dry tongues panting cold, jagged air. In her panic, she flailed off the sofa with a crash. Pain lanced from her elbow and shoulder. She swallowed convulsively as she caught her breath— then, unable to stop herself, logged onto her VPN and pulled up the trap-cameras one by one. The pack remained elusive.

Desperate, she loaded footage from earlier in the afternoon: the family sprinting through a spluttering creek. Their sleek, handsome bodies exuded joy, tongues lolling like smiles. Even in low focus the sight of them safe comforted her. She settled down to observe Kate. The controlled power of her brindled haunches flinging her through the water drew the breath in Sean's chest to an awed standstill. Beautiful but also knowable, the wolf received her world with an openness that included her packmates and her phantom rider, Sean—while asking for so little in return, beyond simple survival. She allowed Sean to be someone else for gulped mouthfuls of time; there was no greater generosity.

"What are you doing?" Riya murmured from behind her.

Sean flinched, staying her hands mid-reflex about to smack the laptop shut. The intimacies she felt watching over her pack echoed, nude and squirmy, as if she'd been caught with late-night porn. Riya leaned to drape arms over her shoulders, chin on her head.

"Is that them?" she said, sleep-raspy.

"Yeah," Sean whispered back.

"They're very beautiful."

The trap-cam flattened forest and wolves alike. Sean resisted the desire to touch the screen; it wouldn't bring them closer. Afternoon sun reconstituted on film glowed incongruously bright in her night-time living room. A protective, possessive emotion washed over her as the recording continued to play, showing her wife her research subject.

"Do you miss her, while you're out of the lab?" Riya asked.

After a tense pause, Sean allowed, "Yeah, of course."

The sciences had drawn her because they encouraged observation from a careful remove, separation from the world as a stance for understanding it—while still allowing her to shape the results that followed after through her own language, her own ideals. Adoring the bigness of life, while dissecting it from a place of quiet solitude. *Except we're not being objective anymore, are we,* she thought. Jealous unease radiated from the warmth of Riya's hands on her chest, while Kate gamboled with her siblings on-screen, unknowing.

A university policeman took Sean's ID in hand, glanced at her face, and waved her through the building's entrance. If the security theater meant her team could get back to work, she didn't mind so much. Three days stuck inside her own skin, cooking, cleaning, and shouting at jumped-up venture capitalists over email hadn't done wonders for her mood. And trap-cam footage, happenstance as it was, told her nothing real about the state of the pack.

"Morning, boss," Christian said from their worktop as she entered the lab.

"Let's get to work." She dropped her messenger bag on the main desk. "We missed a few days of interfacing, but we've got Kate's raw broadcast, so, Alex and Dahye, could you collate that with the trap-cam footage to isolate anything of significance? I'm going to do some footage review also before linking up."

"On it," Dahye answered for them both.

Aseem rolled his chair over to join Sean as the team separated for their labors. His black hair had been given a fresh crop over the abrupt vacation. The close buzz lent him an older edge that his shaggy curls usually softened. Set against Sean's butch, trim presentation, people tended to approach him first, but they both offered variations on the theme of *distinguished gentleman.*

He said, "At least the weather held steady while we were locked out. We didn't lose major data, just the daily baselines we've been building."

With an agreeable hum, Sean opened her ongoing documentation from their cloud server. She also paged through her handwritten journal for comparison to the last interface, wherein she'd experienced twenty minutes of Kate gnawing on an aged bone to test her teeth and whet her appetite. Kate had been *anxious,* if she had to translate the unease to a word she understood. The bone was as cracked and flavorless as the bright, steady winds. The pack understood linear time in a visceral way: cold was coming. Sean glanced at Aseem's relaxed lips, not a smile but a casual expression unpolished for consumption. They had the ease of long-term acclimation, closer to friendship than most of the people in her life.

"I don't appreciate missing that time," she admitted. "Cooperative behaviors are significant, sure, and we'll get there regardless after the cold snap comes—but the data we're gathering now is important too. For the sake of empathy, if nothing else."

Aseem nodded. "Agreed, but our sense of empathy doesn't offer extrapolatable patterns around survival behaviors. What we're getting has been extremely cool, but it basically confirms what we assumed already: animals have minds, feelings; they're not automata. Our grant promises more than that, yes?"

He sounded like a student-facing lecture. Sean grimaced, unable to explain her sudden reluctance to do the work she'd gathered them all together for. On the screen overhead, the trap-cam showed a brindled, adult wolf peering from the tree line across the field. Aseem started to speak but she lifted her hand to pause him. Through the screen, Sean met the thousand-yard stare Kate directed at their camera—or so it appeared, so she imagined. A spark fizzed in her nerves. The tracking dots of the rest of the pack remained near the creek, miles into the forest. Kate had come alone. The wolf sat on her haunches, tilted her head, and yodeled a long call to the expanse of overgrown grass.

"Christian," Sean said, glued to the screen. "Get the machine set up, now."

Regardless of their practice and keen eagerness, fifteen minutes passed before the helmet clamped around her skull. Through the headset, Christian informed her, "Aseem says she's already wandered back into the woods."

Seeing the wolf approach the edge of her territory, coming to the place where they'd first met, had kicked Sean's yearning into high gear. It didn't matter that Kate couldn't know she was there, either on the cameras or inside her mind. Sean missed her and missed *being* her, denied for days the effortless bond strung between their heads.

"That's fine, I don't care. Let's go."

Activation twanged across her synapses; the first rush of blistering scent burned through her sinuses, wildfire-strong. Where branching evolution had dulled her too-human senses, the machine interface resharpened them—or, so she'd journaled, before her enforced break. Piss-marked trees and well-trod paths guided her capable body in a strong lope toward the clustered pack. Air expanded her lungs and rib cage to their maximum with ease. Running made her feel good, free, unburdened.

Motion flicked at the corner of her eye. She pinwheeled, dashed at the rustle. A rabbit burst from its warren ahead of her, but not far enough ahead to escape as she leapt with savage, unhesitating speed. The liquid-lightning transition from casual trot to breakneck chase scrambled Sean's easy occupation of her wolf's psyche. She fumbled, flailing to separate from the depths of their communal self—but not regaining her academic distance before Kate's jaws clamped over the cute furry creature. Bloody viscera filled her mouth as it screamed in agonized terror—wet, coarse, and struggling. Sean's gorge rose. Distantly, she wondered, *what happens if I puke in the machine?*

But even Sean's disgust collapsed under the hugeness of her wolf's satiated pleasure, a dopamine-bliss of success and relief. The rabbit's hind foot thumped spasmodically against her cheek for another two beats before going still. She dropped the carcass between her feet and lay down to eat with delicate nipping teeth. The young sibling hovered hazily in her mind, between imagination and recall. The moment her belly hit *full enough,* she scooped the gory remains between her jaws again.

Which was also the precise second the interface cut, leaving Sean alone in her head. She immediately retched a mouthful of sick-spit at the foul taste coating her tongue, though she knew it was entirely psychosomatic.

Christian ported through the speakers, "You okay in there? Your temperature and your pulse spiked."

"We ate a live rabbit," Sean said, swallowing more drool.

"Oh, gross," they replied.

"But she's about to take the carcass back—could you patch me through again? I really don't wanna miss the first time she brings the kid food."

"The allotted time is over, boss, you need to do the cooldown."

Slick dampness trickled down her jaw. She didn't feel done— and, after experiencing the kill, she sure deserved to see the results. She said, "Just this once?"

Christian said nothing.

"Our protocols are seriously conservative, I highly doubt one more round is going to do me some sort of damage," she cajoled.

"Okay," they responded. "But we're doing ten minutes, tops."

The interface reengaging was more disorienting than Sean expected. The flips from entangled to alone to entangled again spiked through her brain like a needle; she felt its puncture as the sensorium unfurled. Marrow-oozing bones and slippery flesh stretched her jaw muscles, bouncing with each stride, an ongoing delicious savor. As she approached their den, the pup perked up from chewing a stick under the drowsing attention of the mother. His gray-pink tongue lolled out in greeting. Tender grief soured the taste of meat: he was so little. She dropped the rabbit's remains in front of him; the mother met her gaze as he yipped joyously. Sean's own heart seized, beating hard at their painful, communing knowledge as the child stuffed his belly.

The ache helped her recoil, an ounce or an inch, from her perfect union of selves.

Kate sidled over to their mother and nosed against her chin. She rolled onto her side to allow the equally large, equally adult wolf to nestle within the bracket of her long legs. Each chance to be close might be the last. Her thoughts clipped through suffocating *image-recall-smell* of lost siblings. She had no room to be scared for herself with the youngest to watch after. Territory had been bounded on all sides by mowed-down open spaces that rebounded with raucous noise. The waters tasted of metal, and the woods were desolate even before the cold came. No future, none that she or the pack-mother could imagine; nonetheless, they strove toward it.

Christian cut Sean's feed. She emerged trembling, overwrought.

"I need a second," she said to their questioning glance.

They left her to scrub her face with her hands, smearing fresh tears and dried spit. A taut throb of dread crept across her skin. Left alone in her own brain, Sean dredged for her desire to sit back and observe, her desire to *know*, that led to the project in the first place— and found only fear. She had a responsibility, at least, to see her goals through—to preserve as much of Kate for posterity as possible, despite the discomforts: her runty sibling, her aging mother, her hopeful hopelessness. Companion and witness, an unseen watcher through the long nights; Sean could be those things. Spending so long being her wolf, of course she'd come to care for her.

And who else had Sean ever managed such unfettered intimacy with?

Though that thought wasn't going in the official research notes.

Dahye rapped her knuckles on Sean's worktop and asked, "I'm calling out for dinner. You want anything?"

The clock read 6:32 p.m. Alex and Dahye had acres of interface recording and footage to cross-reference and collate for future transcription. Aseem had already left for his dentist appointment, but he'd arrived two hours early that morning to fill the gap. Christian was gathering up their things, as they'd finally finished the last allowable interface session of the day. For the past week the whole team had been going on overdrive, sprinting for lost time. Bruised divots ached at Sean's temples. Waiting for dinner delivery, even if she ate it at home, would have her leaving well past seven for the fifth time in five days.

"Yeah, sure," she said. Hunger from her wolf's stomach lingered in her knotted guts. "Order me, uh, a hamburger? Medium, I guess. And fries."

Dahye's thin brows rose to a comical height. "A hamburger, are you sure?"

Sean shrugged agreement. Dahye laughed, patting her shoulder before returning to the workstation she shared with Alex. The pair haggled over Alex's phone screen for a moment, jostling arm against arm. Seeing their casual, communal touch made Sean's skin tingle. Riya had been distant in the evenings, as if it wasn't reasonable for Sean to work longer hours catching up after the lockout, but no words had been exchanged on the subject. Surely, scrubbing the baseboards and cooking the meals had shown some investment.

"Have you seen they're predicting a cold snap next week?" Alex called across the lab.

"I did," Sean said.

"I told James he should expect me to be in the office, like, twenty-four-seven once that hits. Our baselines are all set, we're ready to see how the cold changes their behaviors," he said.

Sean grunted noncommittally, as she had on each reminder of the coming winter. Transcribing observations from her handwritten scrawl over to the typed, official documents, she paused briefly as she read: *She's worried all the time about the others, and feels—nostalgia, I would call it, or yearning for a better future she knows isn't going to happen. It's almost like fantasizing? And dread too, of inevitability despite the comfort of the fantasy. It's such a complex set of emotions, I almost can't describe it.* On-screen, she typed, the subject maintains a complex awareness of temporality and risk, as in casual group interactions her affects often contain what we might describe as affection but also concern for her packmates, particularly the adolescent male, in consideration of the approaching cold season.

On the cam monitor, Kate and a same-age sibling wove through the trees at the field-line. Under the cover of dusk, with no city lights to intrude, their movement was ghostly—fluid as ripples in water. Sean stopped typing to watch their handsome shadows move before the night vision kicked on, caught between instinctual fear of predators and the *sameness* of having known those paws trotting through the underbrush for her own. The sister-wolf shouldered Kate, as if to nudge her toward the woods. Kate nipped her in return. The pair circled for a moment then melted into the black forest once more.

Another forty minutes of careful transcription passed, largely spent weeding emotion out of her affective observations. No matter the grant's emphasis on sharing and cooperation, on *being in-kind* with her wolf partner, Sean still had to filter the interfaced qualia first through her human physiology and then again through her human language. The neural projections created rough, inexpressible hoards of data; her role as interpreter provided a Rosetta stone for reading that archive effectively. But as she considered the act of translating feelings to words to scholarly prose—stripping loose the emotions—she had to wonder: how much of the humming intelligence of Kate was left in her final product? She reread the last sentence, the subject crosses significant portions of terrain throughout the day, driven to hunt both as an individual and as a member of a familial unit, and recalled her roiling stomach and cramping muscles.

Dahye's phone chimed. "Food's here. Alex, go grab it?"

"Thank god, I'm starving," he said.

"I'll take mine home, I think," Sean mused as Alex jogged off to pick up their delivery. "It's getting late. You should head out too as soon as you can."

"As long as I'm back to feed the cat by eight, I'm good," Dahye said.

Alex returned, food was passed around. Sean popped the compostable clamshell for a sniff of the meaty, fatty burger. Her stomach growled. She glanced up, saw both her assistants looking at her, and closed the box.

"What? I had a craving," she said.

"No judgement here, it's the same thing I ordered," Alex replied, faintly smiling.

"Don't stay too late, I'll need you fresh for tomorrow," Sean reminded them on her way out the door.

The decadent, tempting smell of the burger filled her car. The last time she'd eaten meat had been five weeks after beginning to seriously date Riya, a grilled chicken breast at an Italian restaurant. Nothing juicy, blood-rich. She parked next to her wife's car and considered eating the evidence fast, cloistered in the dim garage. Because Riya was, in fact, home—and surely waiting for her, though she hadn't thought about that earlier. As she picked up the container, the door to the house opened. Backlight framed Riya in warm gold. The pit in Sean's stomach gained three pounds; with a cringe, she slung her bag over her shoulder and slid out of her car. Riya waited for her in the doorway, hands stuffed in her pockets and shoulders squared.

As Sean mounted the steps, Riya asked, "Did you check your phone?"

Her eyes were puffy and red, her lower lip bitten raw.

Sean answered softly, with a sinking feeling, "No?"

"Something happened to Myka." Her voice cracked. She cleared her throat. Sean stood awkwardly shifting her weight from foot to foot on the step below her, because Riya hadn't given ground to let her inside, scrambling to remember who Myka was. "Did you see the news, a fucking superstorm hit Manila—"

Her graduate student. "Oh, hon," she said as the dots connected.

"The whole camp was wiped out. Just, gone. The bay flooded out of season."

"Let's go inside," Sean said.

Riya retreated two steps to allow Sean entry, closing the garage door behind her. The kitchen was spotless: sink emptied of dishes, fresh towels hung from the stove and utensil drawer handles. She'd been nervous cleaning. Riya hovered at Sean's back, silent and still as a ghost as she laid her dinner on the countertop. If she remembered right, Myka was embedded studying climate refugees in the city where she'd been born. As a graduate student, odds were she'd been under thirty.

"I texted you at noon when I found out, to see if you'd come home," Riya said.

Her measured cadence belied the tension pooling within the neat, sterile kitchen. Sean schooled an open expression onto her face and turned to lean against the cabinets. Riya wore sweatpants, a ratty oversized sweater, and her bunny-print slippers; a knot gathered her thick hair on the crown of her head. The outfit telegraphed *soft*, hungry for physical comfort, but her flattened mouth and cried-out eyes countered, *not from you.* Sean remembered tossing her phone in her bag after picking up her morning coffee. She hadn't taken it out again since.

"I realized, I'm not even disappointed. Do you understand? I'd have to *have* expectations for you to be able to disappoint me," Riya said.

"I'm sorry. I didn't see you'd texted," Sean began, her own placating tone grating on her ears.

"The moment you got back to the lab you forgot those couple days of ass-kissing. You didn't even think to text your fucking partner to say you'd be two hours late," she said. "And what's that, did you get yourself dinner too?"

Riya elbowed past her and flipped the clamshell open. Sean opened her mouth to explain she'd just been craving, it wasn't some kind of statement—

"Oh, cool." Riya tipped her chin toward the ceiling. She gulped down a breath so hard Sean saw her throat bob. Without looking at her, she said, "Get out."

"Over a hamburger, really?" she blurted out.

"No, it is not over a hamburger." Riya lowered her head, blinking furious tears out of her eyes. Wet tracks spilled from the corners. "I don't want you here tonight. I don't want to deal with you and this at the same time, and losing Myka is more important. Go be somewhere else."

"Don't be like this," Sean cajoled—but she wasn't brave enough to bridge the seven-inch gap between their bodies.

Riya stepped close and tight, instead, smelling of faded perfume and laundry softener. The emotions shifting across her face, seen from scant inches apart, were miserable and forbidding. Anger seemed to be chief among those feelings; Sean hadn't ever seen Riya this pissed off with her before, as if scales of resignation had fallen away.

"Be like what?" Riya asked, her voice thin and shaking. "I dare you, Sean. I *dare* you to say what you mean, yeah?"

"Maybe you shouldn't be alone tonight," Sean backtracked.

"Funny how you care about that now. I'm not asking again. Get a bag, leave, call me in the morning. We'll talk more then."

Riya turned from her and strode out of the room, without so much as a glance backward. The office door slammed.

Miller, his tail low and his big expressive eyes limpid, padded up and nudged Sean's dangling hand with his snout. Shocky regret pounded her heart against her rib cage. She tossed the uneaten burger in the trash, compostable container and all, before slinking upstairs to stuff pajamas, toothbrush, and comb into her conference weekender bag. The house held its breath as she reversed out of the garage. Her bedroom window glowed like a golden beacon in the cold night.

At the research complex, a handful of windows stood alight across the glass front wall. The late-shift guard buzzed her in without comment. She was far from the only overzealous worker. The to-go bag from a fried chicken restaurant weighed down her right hand, looped over her wrist. She flicked on all the lights to combat the stillness of her spacious, empty lab, then sat at her desk, unpacked her meal, and booted her workstation. Without Christian the interface was inaccessible, and the pack was likely to be sleeping somewhere off-camera, but she had footage and data to review.

Earlier that afternoon, she'd interfaced for a grooming session—her wolves nibbling, licking, tenderly caring for one another's bodies. The recollection of receiving such meticulous attention, the undercoat-rustling scratchiness of grooming teeth, echoed across her synapses. If she cast herself backward with enough focus, her tongue remembered the sensation of fur on its ridges, oily and dust-coated—foreign but comforting tastes for a creature of two minds. Driven by bodily memories, she located the trap-camera footage that corresponded to her memory and pressed play. The first bite of chicken-flesh and grease filled her mouth while she saw herself, or her wolf, on video: brindled coat, shaved scalp now furry again, huge ears and paws. An unexpected dislocation, far worse than hearing her own voice speaking back to her on her phone's answering message, smacked her across the face.

The chicken tender fell from her nerveless fingers. Memories of her*self* experiencing their warm, simple camaraderie ran aground on the sight of an animal recorded by a field camera, another form and creature entirely separate from her. On-screen, the gray wolf she'd designated as *Kate* dragged her tongue across the adolescent's nape and ears while he whined his complaints like a teenager having his face wiped by his mom in a restaurant. Sean's chest constricted. An ugly, nasal sob crawled from her throat. The pack continued grooming unaware as she observed them, data gathered to be viewed in a sterile lab and annotated for future analysis. None of the closeness echoing from her borrowed memories of skinship truly belonged to her.

Bathroom fluorescents washed out Sean's pale face and highlighted her puffy, purpled eye sockets. She'd never put on the pajamas from her weekender, choosing instead to pass out with chicken grease–covered hands in a reclined office chair—and now, was cursed with a wrinkled button-up and sweaty undershirt, indents from her slacks slicing across her hips and thighs. She flicked water off the toothbrush and stuck it into its travel container. Aseem was due in soon. His schedule ran earlier than hers. Before he arrived, she left a message on her therapist's answering machine requesting an emergency appointment. Her second call hit Riya's voice mail; Sean hung up without leaving a recording.

She expected to feel *something* the morning after their blowout—desperation, some combination of fear and guilt—but the main thing she felt was tired. Fighting and making amends, wading across the distance between them just to be swept out to sea again, struggling in sight of land: the ongoing cycles wore her down. Laid alongside the visceral, intimate oneness she'd be tapping her brain into shortly, her marriage didn't measure up. She felt bad that she didn't feel bad. When the lab door eventually opened, Sean met Aseem's startled blink at her appearance and bit the bullet to announce: "Riya requested I absent myself from our house last night. We're, uh, having difficulties."

"Oh," he said, visibly processing. "I'm sorry to hear that. Do you want to talk?"

"Honestly, I just want to work," she said.

"Is that maybe the problem?" he asked with a sympathetic grimace.

"Shit, you know it is."

Sean thumped her skull against the headrest of the chair, slowly, twice. Aseem sat at his station, sorting out his bag, his coffee, and his breakfast in casual silence. He also had a wife: an artist, if Sean remembered right. Surely, if anyone understood her issues balancing the self-centeredness required for success in their field with a functional home life, it would be Aseem. He offered her the Tupperware containing sliced fruit, nuts, and cheese. She snagged a grape and a bite of cheddar.

"I do know, but you should remember you're striving to match an impossible standard other men have set in our field, and that's the problem," he said.

Sean nodded. The drive to prove herself, over and over again, to a system that wasn't designed with people of her—or, even, Aseem's—sort in mind, kicked like amphetamines with as bad a hangover. She'd done a five-star job as one of the guys, though; it had catapulted her to the head of this lab.

"So you also think I'm working too much?" she asked.

"Speaking as a friend, not a co-researcher, you do seem overinvested." Sean sat up straighter as he continued, "You spearheaded this project, yes. But I wonder if connecting your brain to a creature experiencing trauma is encouraging trauma-bonding? You seem to feel close to her, but she can't reciprocate. A bit parasocial."

"Developing our empathy is the point, though," she said.

Aseem lifted his hands in surrender and said, "I'm not talking about empathy, I'm talking about thinking there's a back-and-forth relationship where there isn't one. And if your partner is kicking you out of the house, something is wrong there. As for me, I'm here an hour early so I can leave this afternoon, in time for my wife's gallery. The animals will wait for us. So maybe, think about reshuffling your priorities, yeah?"

But I'd rather be here, working, than home, Sean knew better than to say aloud.

Another grape burst between her molars. Christian wasn't due at the lab until 9 a.m., and it was 8:07.

"Thanks for listening, Aseem. I'm going to go grab a coffee, you good?" she asked.

"I'm fine," he said. She stood and cracked her stiff spine; she'd be paying for sleeping in her chair, for sure. "Sorry this is happening right now. It's very bad timing."

"Thanks," she repeated.

Her emergency session with Jonas, later that afternoon, quickly transformed into a scramble behind her barriers. Knowing she was doing it but unable to act otherwise, Sean offered monotone, flat responses even to his gentle prodding to ask if—just, maybe—the thought of her relationship ending brought her some relief, and why that might be the case. His conscientious questioning and lack of judgement paradoxically made her feel worse than being shouted at for being a terrible partner. At the bubble-tea café she ordered a taro milk with extra boba, face flushed with shame. She hadn't even mentioned that their latest conflict had started with Riya losing a student, because it was no big feat to see who the asshole was in that situation.

"Fuck therapy," she muttered as she checked her phone for any message from her wife.

Nothing.

It was 4:52 p.m., eight minutes before official end of shift.

She texted, *would you like me to come home?* then sat at the corner table sip-chewing her sugar boost. If no response came through before she finished . . . maybe she'd go back to the lab. The whole shift had run off-kilter, her rumpled appearance and shit demeanor throwing the team's energies into disarray; worse still, knowing they'd seen her vulnerable made Sean itchy and irritable. None of them were her friends. She was their professional colleague, and in some cases their direct boss. Of her three allowable interfaces, she'd only used a single one, right after lunch as her wolf napped. Bearing witness to her colorful, almost hallucinogenically alien dreaming had been a raw pleasure—one that eased her queasiness around the parasociality of their bond in the face of her failing human relationships. Immersed though alert, observing the dream gave it a lucid air and a thrilling, vertiginous slipperiness. For a second, she saw the marketing VP's argument for sales potential. Her prose fell short of how strange and wonderful the waking, watchful dreaming had been.

Then Riya responded: *I'm staying with a colleague tonight while I think things over, but please feed Miller on time.*

Sean considered a series of possible questions, like, how was she handling the loss, what was the department doing in response, what would she need from Sean? But instead, she just typed, *okay.* "On time" meant later evening, leaving her another chance to check on her wolves if she acted fast. Sean fired a quick message for Christian to stick around, if possible, and run her through one last session before their shift ended. They responded, *I have to go by 6 sharp but we've got time.*

Funky, aging milk-sweetness clung to the roof of her mouth as she went through the routine of alcohol swabs, restraints, and helmet vise-gripped onto her skull. Anticipation caught her breath in her chest as Christian counted her in, and she smashed through the opening barriers as if through the surface of a still pool. One ephemeral border stood between her mind and her wolf's, between a world of solitary, tired skin and a world of scents, tastes, communing bodies; the helpful machine flung her through its natural resistance. Within her wolf, the evening gloam glowed clear as daylight and approaching night perked her ears, put a bounce in her trot. Sean made a note to herself to arrange a rotation of evening or full-dark observation for when the pack would be most active, compared to the days spent 75 percent asleep—and then, she let herself dissolve.

A shivery tingle flared from their ruff to the tip of their tail. Their howled invitation, vibrating their ear canals and throat, produced a choral set of answers from the ranging pack. However, it was the one closest that sparked a twitch of *intrigue-interest-attention*; she wheeled in his direction, crossing through bracken, burrs scratching at her face. Tail fluffed and neck swung low, she approached him sidelong. He butted heads, cheek to cheek, and caught her scruff between his teeth. The tug of his loosely gripping jaws yanked down into her belly. She shouldered him aside, whining grumpily, but he growled and snagged the flesh in his mouth again. The pressure of teeth zinged, pleasurable and strange. She flopped onto her side, forcing his grip to slacken unless he intended to cause harm, and pawed playfully at him once he allowed her to escape. Struggling for a moment's breath, Sean dragged herself loose from the intense physical sensations—distractedly parsing the mixture of eagerness and almost-laziness as a desire to *fuck*.

Last year the pack had produced no pups, and the season was ripe for mating. The tips of Sean's ears went hot. Their pack already had a leading pair, and her wolf hadn't enticed a mate from beyond the familial unit, but—animals weren't beholden to the rules of people. An abrupt burst of envy roiled through Sean, alongside a shivery, sympathetic arousal. *You don't have to worry about using your words,* she thought irritably at her amused, unaware wolf. The male dropped into a tussle with her—smelling of grassy earth and his own musk, willing to roll through underbrush with leaf-litter clinging to their coats. Once again, he lay teeth over the vulnerable column of her throat. The reverberation of his growl in those muscles made her splay relaxed. Balancing two bodies, Sean's brain pinged between the physical—her pulse climbing, mirrored warmth building embarrassingly between her legs—and the emotionality of her wolf's brief happiness.

But another howl interrupted them; *come home,* the tone said. Kate wriggled loose, an odd mixture of disappointed and unconcerned, and huffed a warning at her packmate's begging whine. Both wolves set off to rejoin their family. Awareness of his presence, padding along devoutly at her hindquarters, banked a slow, steady glow of sexual intrigue. Reaching the den, she nudged her parents' chins and licked their teeth. The unit coalescing with all members accounted for, from father and mother to rangy adolescent to four other siblings, gave Sean and her wolf alike a moment's relief. Looking forward to her night spent in a silent house and a cold bed made her chest sting. *I've never had so many people in my life at once,* Sean thought longingly—her own private feeling, separating her another step from their unified self.

While she seized the opportunity to bask in the presence of bodies surrounding hers, their postures speaking *welcome* and *flirtation* and *I-smell-what-you-were-doing,* Kate proceeded through a gauntlet of chilly noses and friendly nibbles. Sean distantly wished she could remain within the interface all night, and damn the consequences. But as the father tried to nudge his pack into their resting huddle, Kate remained resistantly on her feet. Her attention drifted southward along the track of the blowing, biting wind. The adolescent bumped her with his nose as well. Sean, figuratively, froze and leaned closer to inspect this emotion. Her consciousness floated looser in the feed than usual, as her wolf's tail bristled erect. Kate growled toward the mouth of the den, as if sensing something no one else could see. Before the echoed impulse of not-right faded, before Sean could force herself back beneath the surface of her wolf's mind, the interface cut out and dumped her into her own flesh.

"That's it for the night, boss," Christian announced through the speakers.

"That got weird at the end, I'm not sure what's up with her," she said back.

"I'll have Aseem review the data with us tomorrow," they acquiesced.

Helmet lifted at least, she blinked stars from her eyes. Christian gave her the thumbs-up and left her to sort herself out. Wriggling out of the chair made her uncomfortably aware of a tacky, damp patch sticking her underwear to her crotch. By the time she emerged from the machine room, Christian was bundled in their coat and gloves, tossing her a casual wave on their way out the door—clearly rushing to end their shift. Sean made sure her toothbrush and other haphazard supplies were accounted for in the weekender before hauling it over her shoulder, setting off for her car through the streetlight-banded night.

In bed later, reading glasses on and tablet in hand with a glass of wine on the end table, Sean scrolled the subscription feed she shared with Riya. Headlines like "Superstorm Devastates Philippines" butted up alongside dire scholarship: "Collapsing Ecosystems: On the Nature of Species Extinction in 2031," or "Social Fragmentation and the Privatization of the State: A 50-Year Retrospective." Sean sipped her wine, which was actually Riya's, just for the acrid taste. Her stomach sank onto her backbone as she filled her brain with things larger and infinitely more awful than her own dull, scrabbling life. Mass catastrophes put her failing marriage in scope— and reflected poorly on her experiment in all the ways her wife had pointed out previously.

"Hey boy, Miller," she singsonged. The dog lifted his head and tail simultaneously from his quilted bed. She patted the duvet. "Come on. Up, up."

His tongue lolled out, head tilted. He wasn't allowed on the bed.

Sean groaned and slid out from under the covers to lift his squirmy body. Fur got up her nose. His one snaggletooth bumped her jaw. She dumped him on the bed and climbed on behind, hugging him tight. He huffed, squirmed, relaxed. Her house, her rules.

III

Takeout containers drew a no-man's-land between Sean and Riya, seated on either side of the breakfast nook. Sean served out pasta and salad from their favorite Italian place, bouncing between prey-stillness and vibrating anxiety. Riya had done a full face of makeup, including carmine lipstick, and wore a button-up with a high collar: meticulous and armored. Miller gallivanted in the yard chasing birds and couldn't provide a distraction from their conversation. The season's first snow, with a chaser of freezing rain, was due to blow in overnight, and the lab team had been jubilant. They welcomed winter's encroaching hand, about to squeeze closed around the forest and their subjects. Sean had almost called for an all-nighter, driven more by nerves than necessity, until Riya texted her *let's have dinner and talk tonight.*

"I brought the plants in from outside," Riya said, breaking the stilted silence.

"Thank you," Sean said. "Guess we have to start being careful about the cars' batteries again."

"Mm, and we'll need to have the tires switched," she agreed.

The first rich bite of tagliatelle and asparagus slid over Sean's palate, a kiss of butter and parmesan. Over the last near-decade, they'd eaten together from this place more times than she could count, and the thought of picking over pasta alone and putting half into the fridge as leftovers made her sinuses sting. Relearning single life, her steady domestic companion leaving her in middle age, sounded unbearable. Something had to be better than nothing, but she had a sinking feeling Riya didn't agree.

"I don't want to lose you," Sean said abruptly, knifing the negotiation open.

Riya twirled her fork listlessly in the pasta. "Of course I don't want to lose you either, but—Sean, I've given you so many chances. There's only so many years we're alive on this earth, and I don't want to waste more of mine waiting for changes that aren't going to happen. I'm *unhappy*."

Sean closed her teeth around a rebuttal. They'd raised a dog together, bought a home together; their colleagues respected them as the comfortably married lesbians who hosted good dinner parties and published well-received research from a shared workspace. None of those practical building blocks of a stable life felt to her like "wasted time." How would she structure her days, lacking the support strut of a wife—another person with whom to split her responsibilities? She swallowed a heavy, overly chewed bite of pasta and forced herself to look at Riya, with her hair gathered to a ponytail at the base of her neck and her fork tapping against her lips. Her meal sat untouched. Sean's heart still gave a slow pulse at the sight of her, despite the shambles of their life.

She said, "So what do you want me to do, now? It sounds like you're already working toward—it sounds like you've made a decision."

"Well, I thought . . ." Riya paused to chew her bottom lip. Crow's feet pinched at the corners of her eyes and around the scrunch of her nose, wrinkles that would be cute under better circumstances. "I thought maybe we'd take a break, get some space from the habit of being together. See if I'm, if *we're*, happier apart? Or, if getting back together seems better. And then—then, we discuss about it again."

She slid her phone out of her pocket and tapped it a few times before handing it across the gap. On the screen was a posting for a visiting professorship, termed at two years with the potential for a third-year renewal, at JNU—in Delhi. Sean skimmed the details, a handsome package that fit neatly into Riya's research and allowed closer access to her fieldwork. From a collegial perspective, she knew she should support her wife's application for the position, and it wasn't as if travel and research hadn't separated them for stretches in the past. But then was different from now.

With resignation, she said, "I'm hearing this as an ultimatum. Like, as our marriage stands, you're done with it."

Riya frowned, her fingers drumming on the tabletop. "If you're going to insist on seeing it that way, okay. Just remember, all the shit surrounding your project, I put up with for months and months. And then, what happened with Myka? I can't keep going 'round on this, and I don't want to. You shouldn't expect it. I'm sure there are women who'd be glad to be your housewife, but I've never been one of them, and I didn't marry you thinking you'd age into a patrician whiteboy."

Sean wrung her hands, embarrassed and frustrated. "All right, so no ultimatum, but you're intending to go away—to leave."

Riya's phone, sitting neatly between them, dimmed to sleep-mode.

"Yes, for a while, and if not for this posting then another. Weren't you just saying, I wasn't from here? I've stayed for you, for this house, but being closer to my mother and my cousins sounds good for me, given how things are going." Riya leaned back. "I'm not saying you shouldn't visit me, I'd hope you would be happy to."

Sean forced herself to confirm, "Are you asking me for a divorce?"

Riya sighed, deflating into her seat from the tense, upright posture of her short speech. "No, I'm not."

Not yet, Sean heard lingering underneath.

"You're asking to separate, though," she said. "What will I tell people?"

Riya's mouth flattened briefly; Sean flinched at the hurt crossing her expression like a wisp of cloud cover, knowing she'd said the wrong thing. Her wife responded, measured, "When I struggle with whether our relationship is still good for us, my concern isn't focused on 'what will the neighbors think.' Instead I'm worried, am I going to be able to survive losing this, or will sustaining it be the thing that kills me."

Sean took another bite that grit in her mouth like sand. Wind shrieked outside, a gale rattling the trees; their dog scratched at the back door. She stood to let him inside. Was there no middle ground, no comfortable place between their divergent priorities where Sean could meet her wife—to sustain, as she'd said darkly, a life near enough to what they wanted? Impending years of a cold, empty home and a partner on the other side of the world cinched taut around her throat like a collar. Miller shook himself, toenails tapping on the kitchen floor as he trotted past them without a care in his head.

"Say something, Sean," Riya prompted quietly as she returned to the table.

"I'm not sure what I should say," she replied. "You're clearly miserable with me, but I'm not miserable with you."

Riya set her knife and fork to the side entirely, giving up the pretense of eating with a grimace. She cleared her throat of a soft catch and said, "If it's actually *me* you're glad to be with, and not just a warm body to stand beside you at parties or cook your dinner, this won't be the end. When I'm away you'll miss me, you'll fly to see me, you'll work for it a little."

"Okay, I understand," Sean said, sounding just as strangled.

"But," she continued, steady eye contact with a damp lash line. "I won't be surprised if you don't, and that'll be that. I'm finished with shouldering the whole burden alone."

Sean nodded jerkily. Fair was fair; if she couldn't be fucked to text her wife from fifteen miles away, how would she handle crossing the Pacific and being among strangers on a regular basis? Or getting up at 6 a.m. for video calls while Riya ate her dinner, putting aside the labwork so their morning-and-night chats would match? Those challenges required a whole different form of accountability than remembering to snag a box of anniversary chocolates.

"I've been supporting you, your career, and your feelings, for so long. Can you support me while I pursue some big living, now?" Riya asked.

"Okay," Sean repeated.

"So I'm applying for the position then," she said.

The quilted gray clouds outside the bay windows settled dense, gravid, threatening. Sean said, feeling emptied clear out, "I don't see where I've got much say in the matter."

Riya tossed her hands up. "Sean, I just need you to *try* to keep me."

"I'm sorry, and I swear I love you," she repeated again.

Riya gulped a huge mouthful of her wine. Rain began to patter in a hush outside, droplets murmuring against glass and grass. Sean's wife was brilliant in her field; she'd land the position if she applied. While her own familial unit was casting itself against the rocks, Kate should be nestled closely with her siblings in the den—their pup warmed within the weft and weave of bodies. Each of them numbly, like marionettes, resumed their meal—pasta gone gummy with chill, butterfats congealing. A terrible, wounded desire to slip into Riya's skull and observe her emotions, chase her thoughts while she chewed her asparagus, overtook Sean; instead of being locked away from her insides, coasting across the surface in words and deeds, she wished she could reach secretly into the deepest parts of her. Maybe she'd understand her better from there.

Later that night as Riya lay snoring, hugging her pillow with a pink sleep-mask covering her face, Sean ran her careful thumb down the bumps of her spine. Silky, soft fabric and warm skin slid in counterpoint. Riya wriggled with a dreaming huff. Her round butt bumped Sean's hip. She scooped her closer, spooned against her side, and inhaled the natural scent of her hair. The familiar irritation of long, dense strands stuck in her mouth and up her nose came as a welcome. As nested as their bodies were, a hollow distance ached in her bones—like she wasn't holding her flesh-and-blood wife, but the ghost of a future loss. Rain turned to rattling pellets on the roof. Sean lay awake imagining the freezing open field under a hailstorm, with no cluster of bodies to keep her safe.

Morning brought a city sheeted in ice, glassing sidewalks and welding mailboxes shut. Navigating the neighborhood slip-and-slide in her poorly equipped car, then puttering at twenty-five miles an hour on the freeway, *then* coasting through the blessedly clear entrance of the parking garage had Sean's anxiety high before the workday even began. Christian had already called to tell her they'd be in later than usual. On the cameras, tall stalks of field grass glistened like bright knives. The remaining foliage that had clung through the long fall was stripped to the earth, bare tree limbs dripping icicles. Only the evergreens remained thickly needled, their waxy snowcapped greenery a sure visual cue that winter had arrived, all at once, in an awful gale.

The pack stayed inside their den, its mouth shadowed and impenetrable by the cams—denying Sean the one thing she needed to feel settled after her sleepless night. She paced around the communal kitchen, attempting to sequester her bad mood, waiting for her coffee to finish brewing through its drip-sieve over her mason jar—*and of course it's a mason jar,* she thought with self-deprecation. Pretending patience, she poured another stream of steaming water in spirals across the fragrant grounds. The brown-black surface puckered and cratered. Christian was due to arrive closer to midmorning, after salt trucks and sun cleared the roads.

Ideally, the pack would sleep through the morning too. Thumbing across the soft weal of scar tissue on her temple, Sean reflected gloomily on the inherent restrictions of their proprietary interface; C. R.'s pet technician was the only person trained to run their big fancy machine, for obvious reasons. But with the paired implants, she and her wolf sharing a unique frequency, why was it so necessary to allow a third person to mediate—to manage and restrict their ability to commune? Kate's neural mesh broadcasted twenty-four seven, pouring into a databank that drank it all down, undiscerning. Without the human researcher to pair those loads of sensation, thought, information, and qualia to observed experiences, there would be no parsing the data—Sean herself was indispensable to Chilson-Reed. If they intended to monetize the research data they were receiving, they couldn't do without her—but she sensed an underlying implication, through the form of her handler, that she couldn't be trusted with their technologies unobserved.

"Hey," Aseem said from behind her.

Sean startled, surprised gooseflesh prickling.

"Oops, didn't mean to scare you." He laughed. She gave him a sore glower, in good enough fun, or so she assumed.

"What's up?" she asked.

"Two things. One, if I may ask, how are things at home? And two, when I was comparing the unmediated feed against your field notes before pushing them through to C. R. for review, I found a few spikes in her raw data that aren't accounted for in your narrative. Before I submit the notes, could you cross-reference your journals to see if there's something that seemed insignificant around then, but that might explain the spikes?" He finished with a demonstrative wave of both his hands—encompassing "our overlords require tribute" and "surely nothing of concern" at once.

The reminder of her crushing dinner the night before dried Sean's mouth and tied her tongue. No one else knew what was happening with her and Riya. She certainly hadn't told her subordinates, and outside of work she didn't necessarily have friends.

She stuttered, "We, uh, had a talk. She's applying for an overseas research posting to give us . . . some space to think, she says. She wants to see her mom more. I'd have to travel."

Aseem nodded, open-faced and supportive; Sean guiltily wondered if he'd feel so sympathetic to her if she shared the *rest* of the things Riya had said. "You know, when I placed here, Anu stayed back in LA job-searching for almost a whole year. It's certainly doable, the space might be good. And you haven't been to see her family much, yeah?"

"I guess you're right, it's an opportunity," Sean lied quietly.

He gave her a manly thump on the shoulder, closing their intimate confessional. Colleagues across the board had done their times working apart, given the nature of the job market. But Riya's impending departure radiated a caustic finality for Sean, a fair test she nonetheless anticipated failing. In the empty kitchen the *drip-drip-drip* of her steeping coffee echoed the stuttering repetition of her worries.

Back at her desk, Aseem had left an annotated printout of a spiking, multilayered graph. Like a vinyl record without a turntable and speaker, the interface's raw recording couldn't reproduce the sensations or information on its own, but could be read against timestamps and her own notes to chart similarities between events and spikes in intensity. Locating the precise times in the camera footage, the interface data, her official field notes, *and* her personal transcription took some time, then more to compare them closely against one another. The strange readings—unmistakable on screen and paper in the sharp disarray of the graphed lines—hadn't registered as significant to Sean as she occupied the moment. *A sense of agitation kept her from wanting to bed down with the family, like she could see something in the horizon that made it impossible to relax,* she'd scribbled near the end of her journal entry. The clean, professionalized field notes said simply, before termination of the interface connection, subject displayed agitation. The cause was not located by the researcher.

The agitated peak of her wolf's raw feed hadn't been limited to that moment, though. On the readout, bumps and spikes of various magnitudes began to oscillate through the data as soon as the interface paired, then tapered off once the session concluded. A foreboding discomfort sluiced down Sean's back. Kate shouldn't show any sort of response to their circuit's activation; her neural broadcast should be a steady constant, pouring ever-outward, whether her human was peering through the veil or not. Just as concerning, the lack of correlation between Sean's experiential data and the machine's hard readout revealed a gap between her and her wolf that she hadn't noticed.

Once Sean had taken a moment to scrape her anxious brain off the ceiling where it had flung itself along with her heart rate, she called over to Aseem: "You're right, it's weird. The stimuli appears to map onto our interface sessions, but within the notes I took, there's no special events or sensations neatly matching those intervals."

"I'll keep an eye out for more spikes along that vein," he said. Dahye and Alex had just arrived, settling their things at their desks as he continued, "I have to admit, it's fascinating there's something her brain feels strongly enough to appear in the data but which you were unable to sense or translate."

"Oh, did we find something neat?" Alex interrupted before Sean could defend her intimacy, or apparent lack of intimacy, with her wolf.

"Maybe," she allowed.

"Results require reproduction," Aseem said, only half-joking.

On the trap-cam, one quivering snout poked from the den. Oldest male sibling, Sean noted as he emerged with fluffed tail and bristling hackles. He yawned. Her training said *stress* while her anthropomorphizing instinct said *just woke up*. The pack emerged behind him, prancing on the crunchy cold leaf-litter with flinching feet. Breath fogged in front of their faces. Kate nudged the adolescent along, but he seemed reluctant to face the brisk morning, his ears and tail drooping. Sean's whole body itched for Christian to arrive. She was missing these familial moments, adrift in her own solitary body.

"They really are amazing," Dahye said, approaching at her side.

Sean glanced over. Her assistant stood with her hands in the front pockets of her long green skirt. A fluffy turtleneck almost swallowed her to her pointed chin, fashionably oversized. Her face held soft wonderment, a respectful appreciation—but Sean knew those emotions covered a prurient, anticipatory interest. How could it be otherwise, given their entire project? Their wolves should've been round and fat-thick for winter; instead, their lean bodies struggled for lack of prey even during the warmer months, the forest cut off on all sides from its previous migratory byways by encroaching human habitation. Constant development had costs that weren't going to be paid by the folks waiting out the freeze in their suburban living rooms.

"Watching them sure puts shit in perspective," Sean said—vague enough to avoid suspicion from the rest of the team.

If she were god, she'd draw down an endless golden fall—the liminal time after her communion with her wolf but before the ice arrived to threaten their pack, before Riya decided she'd finished with their holding pattern and began to search for escape hatches. What a shift in priorities, from the prior winter spent writing the grant proposal, heart pounding on 8 p.m. espresso and the hunger to do something *big*. But she wouldn't go backward either, if that meant abandoning the bond with her wolf; she was bringing her dreams to fruition with her own hands.

By the time Christian arrived, the pack had disappeared off-camera to explore their ice-transformed territory, trackers moving perpendicular to the central creek at a sedate pace. Despite her middling efforts at patience, Sean projected an air of pacing intensity, which Christian picked up on with hustle of their own—forgoing a trip to the break room for coffee and heading directly for the interface.

"Weather finally turned, huh," they said, entering their code on the touchpad.

"Mn, there's fresh data for us to gather," Sean agreed, politic.

In the interest of expedience, Sean sterile-wiped the machine herself while Christian prepped their end of things—booting programs, arranging their tools and keyboards. Being strapped down on the chair now relaxed Sean to an almost meditative state, her racing thoughts quieting in anticipation of the oncoming communion. After the week she'd had, having her shortcomings thrown in her face one after another, simply feeling how her wolf felt sounded euphoric. An eager rush pulsed through her guts when Christian counted her down. She'd been longing for Kate, missing the respite of being with her—

—stinging cold slashed at her paws and nose and gums with jagged claws. Sean's guts cramped to a hard, hungry knot in sympathetic mirroring, and she dispersed beneath the weight of her wolf's self. Her pack hadn't brought down a large kill in weeks; they survived on rabbits or birds, on scavenging scraps from old, near-inedible carcasses.

The whines of the adolescent, lifting his feet from the underbrush in prancing discomfort, stabbed at her eardrums—echoing the lingering pain in her skull, the pain from the lost time, after which she'd arisen in a strange place confused and sore. With a distant, ghostly regret, some human remainder of Sean thought, *traumatic recollection of the surgical procedure.* She sandwiched the pup between her side and that of the sibling male, spreading some of their warmth into his thin, fragile flesh.

A sour desperation curdled across the pack's comingled scent, swished by anxious tails and buoyed on wheezing breath. How far could each of them range, and who could sustain it the longest? Daylight hours were warmer than their accustomed hunting time in the gloaming, chill evening. She tasted those group-thoughts on the air, gathered them from minute postural changes as the group wove trotting through the bushes. *Adaptations,* Sean noted, unable to stop herself from a moment's distracted scientific interest. Nothing moved but the pack in the frozen silent wood. Her wolf yipped for attention, guiding the pup to nest beside herself and another sibling on drier ground under the hollow of a fallen tree. The rest moved on with a tail-flick of acknowledgement she read as *keep him warm.* Their pup would adapt as the cold dragged on, and on, and on—or, he wouldn't. He clambered onto her side, pounds heavier than was comfortable, in an effort to warm his tender paws. Seasons change and the good times disappear. Fear saturated the nudge of her jaws against those of her siblings in a bid for small physical comfort, re-membering the terrible losses of the previous winter; fear bled from her pores as a stinking cloud; fear dug nails into her empty belly.

Sean emerged from the abrupt interface cutoff into a black si-lence. She'd gone in thirsting for relief, for distraction, for affec-tion; that wasn't what she'd gotten for her troubles. Christian's hands worked to loosen the restraints, cold brushes against her skin where she burned hot, warming against a false freeze her brain had been pumping into her synapses. Sweat oozed from her armpits and dripped down the crack of her ass. While the physical responses to psychosomatic temperature perception were mildly fascinating, nothing trumped her nauseous awareness of watching harm come to someone she cared about, but failing to intervene. Christian gave her a searching glance as she emerged from under the helmet.

"How was it, in there?" they asked.

"Tougher than expected," she admitted.

"Yeah, I figured," they said. "You're going to have a front-row seat, boss, and it won't be pretty."

"I can handle it," she said eventually.

Christian nodded, but their posture—she knew now to read the shoulders, which did translate between species—blared disbelief. Sean's heart thudded resentful against her rib cage, protesting the wringer she'd just put it through, the heady awfulness of her wolf's fear and desperation, her real love—so much more immediate than Sean's own muddled, resentful attachments.

The grinding, mechanical whir of the garage door echoed Sean's stabbing headache. Though she was a couple hours late back from the lab—she couldn't bring herself, especially after the morning's session, to waste a single moment with her wolf—Riya's car wasn't home either. Sean double-checked her phone, but she had no messages from her wife. She frowned reflexively, heading inside to Miller's eager baying barks and ruffling his ears as her gaze swept the kitchen. No dinner left warming in the oven, no explanatory note on the counter. The paper meal-plan posted on the fridge hadn't been updated since last week, before their blowout fight. Turnabout was fair play, Sean reminded herself, but remained unsettled by Riya's marked absence. Her final interface session, spent with her cold, hungry pack, had eaten the scraps of her emotional bandwidth.

Riya's hoard of healthy-ish snacks from the wholesale store—trail mix, rice crackers, organic gummy bears—sang a siren song. She'd skipped her lunch and nibbled pretzels for dinner. Finding her own appetite, after being washed with her wolf's desperation each time she synced up to the neural feed, was easier said than done; ensconced in her cozy office chair with central heating and access to one hundred forms of carryout, the guilt made her sick. Four years of memories of lost siblings, dead to starvation or frostbite or accidents. Her girl Kate carried a world of hurt in that achingly tender brain. Gummy bears in hand, Sean retired to the couch and turned on the television to fill the space with sound. She pretended that if her wife had come home, she would confess her growing sense of conflict—her regrets for the suffering unfolding in front of her eyes—then nursed a petty, miserable satisfaction that she'd been denied the opportunity.

Aimless scrolling through her contacts showed her the names of colleagues, none close enough to chat with, and her team—far too close. Miller hopped onto the couch, burrowing his snout between her relaxed bent elbow and the cushions. His huffing breath tickled her side, so she reclined to give him room to resettle on top of her, one of her legs propped on the couch and the other splayed off. A scratch behind his ears made his eyes droop.

"We're all you have, huh," Sean muttered.

At twice the age of the male pack leader, Miller had grown to be a distinguished old gentleman, cooped up in a vast human house all day with vacuum robots for company. Neither Sean nor Riya spent enough time with him, not for a herding dog whose energies still ran quick and high. For a moment, she pictured adopting him a pup of his own, but came to a screeching halt when she remembered she was probably a few months away from an empty house and a wife living overseas. No puppies on the horizon, not for her or Miller. If she brought one home now, Riya would accuse her of using the new dog as a bribe. On that grim note, she fired off a quick *what's up?* text to Riya.

No response. The implied rejection stung her pride.

As evening dragged on, she paced between several household tasks without completing any—scrubbing the sink but skipping the toilet, clearing the bristles of one vacuum. When the sugar from the gummy bears began to turn her stomach, she ate a gourmet frozen dinner from the emergency stash. Though she checked her phone with neurotic regularity, Riya never responded. She even began to journal again about her afternoon sessions, circling the same grounds, driven by her fear of time running short as the weather stayed grim and food scarce. Near the end of the entry, she wrote in cramped small font in the margin: *what else can I do but watch it happen?* When that was done, she dragged herself to bed with a lingering sense of having been appropriately punished. Sleep came from boredom more than tiredness.

A dull orange glow spilling from the walk-in closet woke her some time later, well into the depths of night. Sean lifted her groggy head and propped herself up on one elbow, squinting. Riya emerged in her usual silk shell pajama tank and cotton briefs, meeting her eyes once before she flicked the light off without speaking a word. The mattress shifted under her weight, motion in the blinded darkness.

"Where've you been?" Sean whispered.

"Tonight was Myka's memorial service," Riya said.

Sean reached out in the dark to skim her fingers across Riya's collarbone, guiltily corrected from her assumption that Riya had been giving her a taste of her own medicine. With the fresh wound of her wolf's lost siblings sinking through her, their recollections trapped under her tongue, she understood her wife's pain better, and the strain of bearing it alone. When Riya didn't recoil from the touch, Sean flattened her full palm over her chest; she turned on her side, facing Sean, their knees bumping. Sean couldn't make out her expression in the darkness, without a wolf's eyesight, though she drew in the scent of her toothpaste-minty breath. Riya huddled closer under the arm Sean wrapped around her plump waist.

"Are you okay?" Sean mumbled, diction smushed by her pillow-squished cheek.

"No, I'm not," Riya whispered.

The clock's dim blue numerals, across the mattress on Riya's bedside table, read 2:13 a.m. She answered the sore need Riya radiated with physical touch, as her pack would—how she'd been hungering for—tangling their legs together and weighing her down onto the mattress with her full body. Riya gasped a tearless, relieved sob of breath beneath the welcome pressure, heartbeats pounding breast to breast. Sean wormed the arm trapped under her back down to grasp a handful of asscheek, less sexual entree than a necessary grip to press them closer together. Riya looped arms around her shoulders, then clumsily pushed on her head with both hands until Sean acquiesced to the request and buried her face between her tits. The bump of a nipple brushed her cheek through silk. Her wife hiked one thick thigh over the bony crest of her hip—clinging almost to the point of discomfort.

Sean's next thorough inhale made her gut clench as she parsed the scent of Riya's smoke-and-pine perfume, her natural sweat—but also, another smell on her unwashed skin. An instinctive snuffle drew another heady whiff into Sean's nose. Riya paused her aggressive petting of Sean's shorn scalp, either in response to the sniffing itself or to the rod of stiffness flattening Sean's spine as she *realized*. She hunched her back farther, shrugging loose of the gripping hands to shimmy down the mattress—down her body. Thumbs digging against plush inner thighs, she spread her wife's legs, and the scent knocked her back with the force of a punch. The smell of a stranger's sweat, a stranger's bracingly floral perfume. She ran her nose and lips across Riya's stomach to the crease of her groin, chasing the sweet chocolatey richness of arousal hastily cleaned but lingering on her thighs, her belly. An alive musk, the road map for clever kisses; far from funerary.

"Please, yes, you can, I miss you," Riya whispered frantically.

Sean blinked tears from the corners of her eyes and planted her open mouth over clean cotton underwear—over the unshowered invitation of her partner's cunt. Was it the first time, a response to grief and her wife's failure? Had she also needed a body—*any* body—to stroke hers back toward life? Sean peeled her underwear off with a painful, twisting desire burning at the root of her tongue. Writing over the stranger's claim with her own spit, she gave a sloppy, long lick across the seam of her wife's cunt—refreshing the dried slickness of whatever came before. Riya combed strong fingers through her hair, their wedding band catching short strands as she cupped her hands at the base of Sean's skull to hold her firmly, as if she might stop before she finished. Sean's skin crawled, insulted but aroused, sinking beneath the satisfaction of being handled—of being shown her place.

No work on Saturdays, per team request arranged through Aseem and approved reluctantly by Sean. Outside the kitchen window, flecks of snow fluttered merrily to the ground. The first flush of ice from the last storm had begun to melt off, intermixing with the new flurries to form slushy ground cover. Sean stood by the window, sipping her coffee, while Riya puttered at the stove. A fresh purple lovebite showed over the collar of her robe, left in the animal struggle of fucking they'd descended into the night before. In the morning light, though, her posture kept an embarrassed distance, as if the pair of them had transgressed each other. Sean kept her mouth shut because she wasn't sure how far she'd get in conversation before asking *who else did you fuck yesterday?* Even the jealous hunger of the night before had dispersed, hangdog sadness left in its wake.

"I'm going to meet Myka's parents for coffee today," Riya said over her shoulder.

"Okay," Sean replied, prodding at the psychic bruise of *she might be seeing the other woman* in curious detachment. "Will you be home late again?"

Riya's hand on the spatula flexed, the tiniest twitch. "I'm not sure, I'll see how it goes. Do you want your eggs scrambled or fried?"

"Scrambled is fine, thanks," she said.

The snow kept coasting down from the blue-white sky overhead. Given enough time and effort, those gentle drifts would blanket the landscape. The unsweetened coffee blended bitter with her morning breath. She hadn't brushed her teeth or washed her hands before passing out again the night before, and the remnant funk of dried come pricked her nose with each fresh sip. Distractedly, Riya dropped a plate of eggs on the table for her then escaped to finish her daily preparations. Sean snuck Miller a nibble of her breakfast.

"You wanna go to the park later?" she cooed to him, his ears perking in response.

Riya left a few minutes before ten with a peck on the forehead and no eye contact. Sean dressed herself in HEATTECH from neck to toes, jeans and a flannel on top. The outfit made her silhouette ambiguously masculine: cropped hair and strong jaw, flat chest and narrow hips with a roll of midfifties belly. Miller submitted to his foot-safe booties, a jaunty bandana, and his padded chest harness. His tail swished merrily throughout the process, paws *taptaptap*ing on the hardwood as he paced. Travel mug in hand, Sean clipped him into his back seat harness and set off.

At their usual dog park, wind bit her face red as Miller cavorted with a beagle and a big, awkward Labrador puppy. She stood with her hands stuffed deep in her coat pockets; the other dogs' owners kept their distance. All three watched their pets bond from different vantage points, close enough to intervene if needed but far enough to maintain some privacy. As if to say, *they need this but I don't.* Miller's loose posture, haunches up and front half bowing to invite the puppy to tussle, radiated joy. He'd led a good life, and had at least four or five more years of it to spend with Sean and Riya—or, she thought grimly, with one or the other of them. Compared to her underfed, scarred, overworked wolf, his luxurious life seemed unfair. The snow flaking down from overhead was a curiosity for him rather than a threat, because he had Sean to care for his needs, to tie little shoes on his feet.

"Come on, Miller," Sean called once his buoyancy started to flag. His tail wagged in slow sweeps, tongue lolling.

"C'mere, boy," she said with a snap of her fingers.

He trotted over, saliva frozen in gross strands across his scruff and muzzle. Sean wrinkled her numb nose. Spit was a part of getting intimate. She didn't want to be alone, but Miller would certainly sack out the moment she got him in the house. If her team refused to come in on Saturdays, and her wife was spending her hours else-where, she could at least watch the field cameras on her laptop to pass the time—watching over her wolf, in the absence of *being* with her. Neighborhood streets passed sedately by. When she glanced at the back seat, she saw Miller had already fallen asleep curled in a semi-circle, safety-clipped leash leaving just enough slack for him to rest.

On impulse Sean turned from her usual path, following the signs for the interstate. No one would know, or care, what she got up to for the afternoon. But fifty minutes into the drive, once the country lane shifted to dirt track, she came to her senses—remembering the muddy ruts she'd encountered last time. She pulled to a stop and threw the ecofriendly compact into park. The dirt track ran another two miles or so, to the edge of the field where the mobile surgery had parked. Miller lifted his head and yawned, tail flopping twice.

Maybe she could take Miller for a brisk stroll in the woods, and just—show up on the trap-camera, provoking a hell of a lot of ques-tions and breaking several of her research protocols. Sean clenched both hands on the steering wheel, staring out over the sparkling grasses. The fields had been overfarmed with soybeans, then retired from active cultivation while the soil recovered over several years. Otherwise, the pack might've already been driven off by farm ma-chinery and human interference.

She knew how close her pack must be. A thin, electric thread seemed to throb between her brows, the stitched webbing tying their minds together: Sean to Kate, and Kate to Sean. Without the interface, she couldn't throw their circuit open. She rolled the windows down a few inches. Her nose couldn't sense anything but cold clean air, but Miller went stone still and his ears lifted to their full tufted height. A deep, chesty bark huffed from him.

One baying howl floated from the distance, the bare ghost of a sound tickling Sean's weaker hearing. Hair prickled across the nape of her neck. Fighting his harness to stand to attention, Miller woofed again, and she executed a three-point with haste. He maintained an erect stance despite the bounce and sway of the dirt track disappearing behind them, at attention, listening for another cry.

Dahye tapped her screen to zoom in on something at the corner of one of the trap-cams' feeds. "Look at this, here."

Sean peered at the blurred, enhanced image: a stocky leg with a paw the size of a dinner plate, small rounded ears and short snout. Dahye resumed the footage and the black bear turned away, disappearing into the underbrush.

"Shouldn't bears be hibernating by now?" Alex asked.

"This is way past their usual time, yeah," Dahye responded. "It should've bedded down in like, early November. Since we've never seen it before, it has to be ranging past its usual territory too."

"Food scarcity hits the whole ecosystem," Sean said.

"Maybe this will be our opportunity for a breakthrough," Dahye said.

Sean reached over her shoulder to replay the footage. Without a full view of the animal, she had no sense of its weight or health. A stone of concern settled in her belly. Bears and wolves generally treated one another with antipathy, but the pack had shown novel cooperative behaviors in the past—she'd suggested in their grant proposal that their research would show animals in the process of agreement. *In times of crisis, it's better to work together than to compete.* Philosophically, she'd hoped to demonstrate emotions or instincts prompting nonhuman animals to be vulnerable with one another, to bond cross-species with a facility humans had seemingly lost during the collapse—but personally, the desire to *feel* those intimacies, to slip from her isolated body and meld into her wolf's familial, communal attachments, had eclipsed those intellectual designs. The team's excitement to shore up the project's lagging results filled her with both interest and dread.

"I wonder what will happen if they meet," Dahye said with a bounce in her seat.

"I guess we'll see," Sean replied.

She sorely needed the simple affections of her pack. Christian hadn't arrived at the office, though, and so she had to continue listening to the team's ghoulish chatter about the cold snap, the bear, and their hopes for the wolves' oncoming tribulations. But she'd hired them for precisely this, and ghoulishness paid her mortgage; ghoulishness got results. Riya would say *I told you so*, and just imagining that firmed her resolve. She was a scientist. She could manage her identification with her subject, could draw compassion from it even, while producing objective work on the natural system the pack represented. She'd spent enough years lecturing on methods for maintaining appropriate emotional distance from experimental subjects—she wasn't a first-year crying over voles. And what else could she really do, aside from giving the wolves her full compassionate attention?

Working through the conundrum, she fiddled with her stack of journals. Antsy brain, antsy hands. To Aseem, she finally said, "As soon as Christian gets in I'll do the first session for a baseline while the pack's on the move—then we'll wait for an opportunity. Either with the bear, or if Kate ranges off on her own again."

"That's the behavior that's been fascinating me, honestly," he replied. His cursor flew across the screen, drawing up various data points he'd isolated over the past week, their wobbling peaks and explosive splashes of color spread across several time-stamped sections. "I'm trying to correlate the raw data with what's happening when she separates from the group, because it appears to be a novel behavior, based on the field team's notes from the last two years. Whatever is drawing her aside and causing these spikes in her neural patterns, it's a fresh issue."

Sean twinged, remembering the last time her wolf-girl had been anxious—the specter of pain, disorientation, that she associated with the fields. "Well, it was minimally invasive, but—we did drug her, abduct her, and perform surgery on her. She has experienced, hmm, sort-of image memories, bad affects, around the field."

"A post-traumatic stress response, you're thinking?" Aseem clarified.

"Not dissimilar," Sean said. "Though of course I'm hesitant to, you know, diagnose an animal by the DSM."

"Nonhuman being," Aseem corrected with a small smile.

Though she refused to speak the possibility aloud, she wondered if maybe the sessions were doing—*something* to Kate's head. The first attempt at a procedure like this was bound to produce unexpected results. Sean wished she had a greater familiarity with the technical aspects of the C. R. interface—but fat chance of them giving her the gritty schematic details she'd need to unpick the potential for reverberation—or, mutuality. They'd insisted there was no chance of that, but she had her doubts. At such a critical time in her relationship with her wolf, though, as her mastery over the psychic experience settled, she didn't intend to prod C. R. too much and risk jeopardizing her sole access point.

Cross-species contact happened sooner than Sean hoped: midafternoon, after her second session. Alex alerted the team of the pack's approach to where the bear was last sighted. She strapped down to wait for the final session of the day, eager to observe first contact and tense with adrenaline. During her previous interfacing, Kate's sore, cold joints and general agitation had given Sean a snappish edge—hungry for something to happen. When Dahye and Alex confirmed the pack's approach, Christian dropped her through the surface of Kate's brain: instantly, she was the one with raised hackles, breathing deep into a barrel chest. Her nose, tracking the stink of a strange, large mammal, blazed danger in all-neon intensities. The pack leaders, mother first, cautiously followed the scent's trail through the forest.

She smelled no cubs, no mates. A solitary body against the wind and rain, contrasting with her own companionable group. The adolescent quivered with each step, his tail spiked. Their brother huffed a warning at him, and her tense haunches relaxed fractionally when the other sibling nipped at the youngest—herding him back toward the safe den. Though she and her parents and other siblings maintained the trail, two of the pack would be protected from the consequences. The female leader's ears twitched, swiveling on her head; she too heard the crunch of frozen leaves under a weighty body. Her leaders' postural shifts telegraphed unease and awareness of bellies underfed. Heart-pounding, jaw-clenching nerves. Sean surfaced from their immersion unintentionally, a swimmer breaking water to gasp. Remaining dissolved inside her partner's head, instead of watching from a safer remove, was for once a struggle. At the same time, she felt she owed it to Kate. If watching and recording was all she could do, then *feeling* as deep as possible was her responsibility.

Their body hurt: one cracked toenail stung fiercely on the cold hard turf, and her stomach cramped with roiling hunger pangs. The bear smelled bad; the bear smelled of meat; the bear smelled of potential. Overstimulated by the stench, her salivary glands pulsed. The mother's head tipped low and her tail flattened, belying her uncertainty. Through the trees, she spotted the galumphing creature—scouting for weaknesses, from those massive forelegs to its starved-lean rib cage. The male leader melted into the undercover to flank behind, while the female sidled closer to the intruder. Not too close; not close enough to present a threat or a challenge, though her muscles were strung tight as bowstrings in preparation for either. The bear groaned warning, on sight of them. Her head swayed. Broad shoulders rolled as she drew up partially onto her hind legs. Her wolf's slobbering mouth dripped onto the ground. She was so hungry.

Instead of baying for the hunt, though, her leader yipped a strange call and pranced a slow circle outside the bear's reach. Her loose, low posture remained as neutral as possible, as if offering welcome to a young wolf ranging into their territory for a mate—wary, willing to defend, but far from initiating violence. Sean choked into psychic disorientation, separating once more as Kate's irritated desire to contravene her leader and go for the throat built. Hungry mouths needed filling, and the bear would scavenge food from their hunting grounds they couldn't afford to lose. At minimum she felt the bear should be driven off, but the head female wasn't doing so. She rankled at the perceived inaction—but Sean, unable to relinquish her observational distance, found their disagreement coolly fascinating. The bear eyed them, nostrils flaring. Her belly radiated vulnerable heat, thin skin over greasy organs. The siblings kept their distance with Kate as their tails bristled, teeth itched to sink in—waiting, hoping for a signal. Sean understood, at once, jolting: *the interspecies cooperation isn't group instinct, it's the group following leadership.*

The bear settled onto her hindquarters in an indifferent posture, and the lead female eased closer, ears piqued. Her wolf didn't understand the risk being taken, or why. The bear's darting eyes bounced from the approaching mature wolf to the three siblings forming a semicircle around her. Unlike Kate's intimate understanding of the anxious wolves to her left and right, she shared no common language with the bear. She understood how the big thing on her turf must be suffering—sure as all things, during the cold season—but felt no sympathetic response, only a calculation of worth: her and hers, first. Something about those calm, easy equations allowed Sean to release herself another fraction, to merge into their certainty, their determination for survival. The lead female lifted her snout, flashing a smile of teeth, and edged another foot nearer their intruder—seemingly, offering a sniff, a nudge.

The bear lurched forward in a blur, smashing her shovel-scoop paw into the mother's shoulder in utter silence. Blood sprayed the slushy snow; a curdling, agonized shriek covered the sick thud of impact as she landed, spine-first, against the bare bough of a tree. Her rolling eyes flashed as white as the bone protruding from her flayed foreleg, hazy with terror and rage. The bear roared weakly, rearing onto her hindquarters again—and from the shadows, the male leader leapt onto her unsuspecting back. His jaws clamped over the side of her throat, paws scrabbling to grasp around her thick torso. One sibling dashed to their mother, whose screaming cries echoed jangling in their ears. The bear shook herself with a frantic bellow, slinging the male's bodyweight against the strength of his own teeth buried in her flesh. And she—her wolf, herself in the truth of the fray—snarled the rage from her guts and made a suicidal dive for its hanging belly, between its sweeping claws—

"—Sean!" Christian shouted through the speakers, over the guttural yell she felt tearing at her own throat.

The feed had snapped closed. Sean struggled against the padded restraints, hands clawed and legs straining, the spittle-flinging bear still painted over the backs of her eyelids. Adrenaline pumped hard into her bloodstream. Christian pinned her sternum flat with their palm, clumsily unlatching the headgear and wrenching it free with less care than the multimillion-dollar machine deserved. Their gray eyes bored into hers, panicked.

"Are you okay? Talk to me," they said.

Sean tossed her head back as she gasped for breath, sweat dripping from the bristle of her hair. She ground out, "Patch me back through, you've got to—"

"Absolutely the fuck not," Christian barked, grabbing the underside of her jaw to tilt her head back down toward them.

"You don't understand!" she shouted.

Christian trapped her skull against the seatback, their grip on her head shockingly stern and intimate; she almost tried to bite them, on instinct, as they tugged one eyelid then the other up to check her pupils. When they used their thumb to measure the rabbiting pulse at the side of her throat, she dug her teeth into her own lip instead—fighting the urge to struggle under the clammy fingers gripping the bones of her face. Lancing pain throbbed at her temple, increasing beat by beat until it radiated through her eye sockets and sinuses. She squeezed her eyes shut against the dim lights overhead. Christian held their thumb over her pulse, stiffly waiting for the rate to slow.

"She's—you have to let me in to check on her, she—" Sean mumbled through the constriction of their hold.

"You're in shock," Christian said, measured. "Your temperature crashed and your vitals went haywire. The interface is not designed to chemically traumatize you, which I am one hundred percent sure it was doing."

"If you're not patching me back in, then fucking let me up," she snarled, finally tossing her head and torso in an effort to dislodge their hands.

"Sorry, boss," Christian said—releasing their grip, but leaving her tied down as they leapt to the door and threw it open. "Triage, team, get in here!"

Humiliated, breathing hard from restriction and panic, Sean bared her teeth at the flurry of noise on the other side of the door. Aseem jogged in, still in the middle of rolling his sleeves up. He also checked her pulse, with a more deferent touch, but her building impotent rage had her glowering as he—wincing, apologetic—repeated the pupil test. The assistants loitered around the doorframe, staring.

"Would one of you do your fucking job and check her tracker, instead of standing around gawking?" she said.

Alex flinched. "Hey, shit. No need for that, dude, I'm on it."

Dahye left with him. Ten seconds later, Christian tapping on their machine and Aseem holding Sean's bound, sweat-slimed hand, she shouted, "Kate's tracker is active and moving away from the location, as are all the others except—the oldest female, who's remaining behind?"

Christian and Aseem glanced at each other across her body. She blew a long breath out through her nostrils to keep from screaming, which wouldn't be much more undignified than her current bondage. A rift gaped under her breastbone. GPS dots couldn't show health or wellness, sterile as her official field notes and insufficient to tell her if her wolf was hurt, if the mother was dead, *if.* After another moment she said with deceptive coolness, "I'm calm, and I would very much like you to untie me, thanks."

"Sorry for that," Aseem conceded as he unbuckled her ankle restraints.

"What happened in there, if you can tell us?" Christian asked.

"The mother was attempting to communicate something with the bear, and the bear attacked her. The wound was severe, I assume fatal, but I can't be sure. At which point the male lead and Kate engaged the bear in conflict," Sean narrated, performing the necessary detachment from the thumping awfulness of having lived through the horror.

"Not the information we hoped for, but useful information," Aseem said—his tone so, so gentle.

If she hadn't been cuffed to the chair, she'd have throttled him. Reducing her loss to information—a vicious intent surged through her, animal and real. On the tide of that rage she insisted, voice steely, "I need to interface again."

"No," Christian said, their flatness so direct and serious it gave even Sean pause. They continued, sounding strained, "The chance of me breaking protocol right now, given what just happened to your brain, is less than zero. I need to explore the data in serious detail before we hook you up, *if* you hook up ever again. If the interface is fucking up your brain with traumatic chemical overdose—this is over, full stop. Do you understand me?"

"How long will your review take?" Sean asked.

"I'll work as fast as I can, but at minimum a couple of days. I have to contact C. R. and compare notes with whatever I dig up here," they said. "If our human trials produced this kind of shit, I wasn't ever made aware of it."

"We don't have days to waste," Sean balked.

"You do if I say you do. You're behaving erratically right now," Christian said.

"We won't lose much over a few days," Aseem agreed. He, finally, unlatched the wrist-cuffs. "And I believe you should spend those days recovering. As a fellow professional, if *you* were treating you right now, it's what you'd advise."

Christian interjected, "Can your wife pick you up? Let's be cautious about, uh, driving or operating machinery."

Tersely, Sean said, "No, I'll get a cab. I'll watch the cameras while I wait."

She allowed no room for argument. Being overruled in her own lab, cut off from her wolf and her labor, made her sick to her stomach. If her team were going to mutiny and block her from her wolf when she most needed to be with her, then visual confirmation would have to suffice. As if summoned, Dahye popped her head around the doorframe.

"They killed the bear and are dragging the carcass to the den. Kate's okay, it looks like," she said.

"Jesus," Christian muttered, the rapid-fire clattering of keys wedging into Sean's eardrums. Her migraine ebbed and flowed in waves. "Get that cab and be ready to have some scans taken tomorrow. I'll schedule appointments for you over at med campus."

Sean gnawed savagely at the inside of her lip to keep from snapping *I'm in charge*. None of her team were going to let her direct them at the moment. On a rational level, she understood. But the compounding senses of violation and loss—within her pack, at her office, even in her marriage—left her reeling. Aseem placed an unobtrusive hand under her elbow as she stood, trembling, for a stiff-leg walk to the main room. Claws swept toward her face behind her eyes with every long blink; her skin ran cold with fear-sweat and goose bumps. The team congregated on the other side of the lab, out of earshot, while she collapsed into her office chair. Alex cast her a clipping, concerned glance over Christian's shoulder.

A pair of tracker dots sat unmoving on her screen, far from the den and the gristly lean meat the siblings had dragged there. Elder male, remaining with his wounded—or, worse, already dead—partner for the last stretch of their short, miserable lives. Even at the end, her lead pair refused to separate from one another. The pack's bellies would be full for the night, and the freeze would keep the meat for longer, but the cost was too high. Angry tears budded at the inner corners of her eyes, and she dashed them away. Aseem murmured instructions to the assistants. When the rideshare app pinged, she snatched her messenger bag and stormed from the lab as powerfully as she could.

As the driver signaled his way out of campus, respecting her brooding silence, she texted Riya *will you be out tonight?* before shifting to her thread with the lab team. The last texts in that group message were about meeting at the bar to celebrate their first successful interfaces—their big break. Her stomach flopped. Instead of texting the team, she entered Aseem's number and tapped out a fresh message every few minutes, to no response:

> Update me on the decisions you're making in my absence
> Especially the ones about me
> Have you set up the scans to assess potential damage & clear concerns?
> Without the interface linkage functional, we're repeating the bio team's work & losing time
> I'm still the head of this project, regardless of any distress about the incident

When the final message also went unanswered, she locked her phone but refused to pocket it. The driver turned onto her street. The muscles in her shoulders and torso clenched at maximum tension, to the point that her ribs crunched gently when she breathed. Sharp pains spiked through her skull, down the left side of her neck. As she tried to stretch her jaw, it cramped so hard she grunted and clutched at her throat. The driver glanced at her in the rearview mirror. She waved his concern off, tipping extra when she got out at the front of her driveway. After unlocking the front door she sent one last message to Aseem: *I'm fine, and this is starting to feel disrespectful.*

Miller's usual haywire barking greeted her before he rounded the corner to the foyer, nails skittering across the hardwood. Sean took a knee, messenger bag thudding on the ground. She buried her hands in his scruff and hugged him, toppling onto her ass when his wriggling overbalanced them both. His rough tongue swept over her cheek and nose, processed–dog food breath rancid. She nudged him aside after a moment, then called out, "Riya?"

No response. She double-checked her phone, on the ground. No one had sent her so much as a read receipt for her messages. The grotesque flash of gristle and bone on the mother wolf's flank, her desperate yowling screams, shook across Sean's brain. She hadn't even been there to bear witness in the end, but she hoped her girl was the one who made the kill. Soaked in gore, had she gone to lie by her mother's side—had she pressed their damp noses together to comfort her through her pain, or if she had already passed, to grieve?

Sean had no idea. Emptiness sucked along the suture-line of their severed connection, as if someone had torn her memories loose at the root. She had abandoned Kate at a pivotal moment, left her all alone and returned to a safe suburban homestead with a well-stocked fridge and temperature control. *Monstrous.* All her endless protests about being in-kind or empathy or solidarity rang inside her skull as impotent, selfish fantasies. She couldn't forget her own burst of distancing curiosity, before the worst, the moment when she'd wanted to see what would happen.

Sean tossed her messenger bag into the study, then detoured to the bathroom to swallow a handful of headache pills with water from the faucet. Her reflection in the mirror was gaunt, the eyes sunken and owlish, jaw muscles flexed in stark lines. The thicket of fine hair that had grown over her scarred temple was threaded with gray, as she hadn't yet dyed it chestnut to match the rest. She scrubbed wet hands from her chin to the crown of her head, the longer portion of her hair standing up straight for a moment before flopping to disarray. Her phone buzzed, once.

Riya's text read, *I'm going out for drinks with colleagues, I'll be home late.*

Sean sipped one breath through her mouth, forced it out slowly through her nose, before returning to the study and her laptop. Her VPN access was still unrestricted, which was a resentful relief since the team might've done any number of things to enforce her break while she wasn't there. Camera feeds proliferated on her small screen in tiled array. None of them caught footage of the fight, or showed their progress through the woods with the bear's carcass. According to the feeds, their woods were as empty as a graveyard. Sean needed so badly to see her wolf, her siblings, her pack—instead of glassy, frosted trees and underbrush, their dull muddy browns and cracked golds, green life all absent.

"Fuck," she blurted into the silence.

The impermeable barrier between their minds taunted her. Electrical signals pulsed into nothingness without a breaker thrown to connect them. Sean folded her arms on top of the desk chair and laid her head down, thinking in sludgy circles. Maybe an hour had passed since the confrontation. Ordering a cab to campus to collect her car, purchasing some supplies, and trekking out to the field would take another two at minimum, barring however long it would take to haul materials across the grounds her car wouldn't cross. Five hours was too long to be of any use for the lead female—people bled out in minutes from wounds like that—but she had to do something to help with her own hands. Her sought-after "cooperative survival behavior" might as well run from human to wolf, no matter what her grant proposal said. What else was she, really, but another animal body afraid of being alone in the cold?

IV

Sean packed her trunk in haste: a child-sized drag sled, bags of basic medical supplies—disinfectant, bandages, suture plasters—and a couple hundred dollars' of raw beef from the meat counter. In her frazzled grab for anything that seemed useful, she'd also bought two containers of dog vitamins. The extra-dense muffler and hiking gloves were for her, but if her plan to engage the pack went off the rails, the cold wouldn't be her problem. She collapsed into the driver's seat and cracked open her bottled tea to swallow a double dose of painkillers, trying to stave off the white-hot pulse behind her eyeballs for another hour or two. Cloud-dusted, slate-gray horizon beckoned her out of the parking lot, away from the anonymous bustle of human bodies.

GPS directions rolled out of the speakers in a soft femme baritone. A barrage of text notifications scrolled across her phone screen, but she ignored them. If her wife or her team had responded earlier, she thought vindictively, maybe she wouldn't be driving to the middle of nowhere with a month's supply of meat. The pack needed her more than the humans in her life. Kate hadn't been the one to leave her or betray her trust.

Time melted to a syrupy drag. On arrival to the dirt-track split-off, she discovered the frozen-solid ruts were more navigable than they'd been as raw mud in the fall. She jounced the subcompact over hillocks and around crevasses, teeth rattling, and ultimately parked near the grassless patch where the mobile surgery had stood. The cameras would capture her, but she doubted her staff would've remained in the office without her flogging them into it—and if someone observing wanted to stop her, the drive would still cost them an hour.

"This is fucking nuts, bud," she muttered, removing meat and medical supplies from their packaging as she loaded up the sled.

Hearing her own voice was startling. The words dropped like stones into the deceptively still lake at her center, sending ripples through her emotions. Blood from the beef clung to her new gloves.

The quiet shellacked across her brain was a lie, but her decision to break the barrier between herself and her pack stood firm. Where else could becoming, or being in kinship, lead? She'd been too focused on observing from her comfortable remove, stripping out the feeling from her journals in favor of prim mechanism. To throw over her own proposals, to get her hands dirty: those were material amends. In her pocket, the phone vibrated nonstop. She stripped off a glove, wind biting her fingertips, and flipped the ringer to silent as she read *Aseem* on the screen. Before she stuffed her phone back in her pocket, she read *The neural spike correlation in the email I just sent is extremely concerning . . .*

Rope dug into her forearms and across one shoulder as she hauled the sled over chunky, icy grass. Muscles bunched and burned inside her shoulders, her ribs, her abdomen. She nudged her muffler down to her chin to puff out gasps of steaming air that froze onto her cheeks. After another few minutes of slow progress she staggered to a stop and reconsidered, then turned her ass toward the trees, looping the ropes behind her elbows and grasping them with both hands. She dug her heels into the ground and used the power of her hamstrings and glutes to drive backward, legs catching fire. The sled crushed a singular crop circle through the field. When amplified by the ghostly, borrowed subjectivity whispering within her memories, the boundary-line of trees called to her with the same ferocity as her front door after a long night at the office. Under the trees the air would be warmer, and still; the pack's scents marked the paths, their feet treading the loam.

And maybe—maybe, if some part of them recognized some part of her, her fragile unfurred skin could bed down within their companionate nest of bodies. Longing colored with agony rolled through her, the desire to cross from silent witness to welcomed partner. She *knew* them, and finally, she felt willing to be known in turn.

The first flash of glowing eyes from the depths of the wood, though, froze Sean through animal instinct. Hair rose on the nape of her neck. The rope slipped loose from the backs of her arms, resting slack on her palms. Her eyes only let her see the outline of the wolf through the shadows of the forest, but she remembered how much clearer they would be able to see her. Staring resolutely at the wolf's flank to avoid challenging its wary stare, Sean trucked forward another two steps. A reedy, warning growl trickled from her right, past the barren trunks of trees.

Sean dropped to her knees, discarding her looming human height, and bared her teeth to signal *friend*—another learned behavior. Spreading them so broadly cracked her chapped, dry lips in stinging lines. A southerly breeze whistled from behind her. The smooth, loping patter of paws approached from the forest a scant few yards from her. Sean maintained an unthreatening gaze at the ground, cataloguing the smells of blood from the beef, blood from her lips, and her own acrid fear-sweat in her nostrils. Icy grass stabbed at her shins as she shifted minutely. The flash of terror she'd felt before the first interface session returned, sudden awareness that a gruesome death was on the table. But after the bear—she had to do something.

Despite her fluttering hope that Kate would be the first to approach her, the male sibling with the gray snout and docked left ear took the plunge. He sidled alongside the sled with his tail bottlebrush-bristled to snuffle at the pile of meat. Having scented nothing amiss, he clamped a pot roast in his jaws and retreated two body lengths from her crouched form, maintaining a wary posture. Sean's skeleton was shaped wrong for her wolf's language, and she couldn't control the pounding anxiety carried on her sweat-stink. Her lips and teeth hurt from exposure, but she didn't dare relax her facial muscles. While she waited, shivering, the female sibling emerged from the forest, perhaps drawn toward the tearing, slobbery sounds of her brother's feast. She crossed beside him, nudging his cheek with hers—he huffed over his beef in warning—before approaching Sean herself.

Her ears, held aloft, practically quivered with distrust. Sean strained her grimacing smile wider, craning her head farther forward. The sibling with the pale cornflower eyes edged close, and then closer—near enough for the scent of her oily fur, both like and monumentally unlike Miller's, to creep into Sean's nostrils. Risking a glance, Sean saw the wolf's nose flinching in turn as she drew in Sean's own scent; another foot closer, close enough for contact. As big, yellowed teeth loomed beside her cheek, she had to close her eyes on reflex to keep from whimpering—before a slippery, rough tongue licked across her teeth and gums. Carrion-taste filled her mouth. She swallowed convulsively against her gag reflex, huffing desperately through her mouth to continue receiving the greeting. Another quick, darting lick painted slimy saliva across her philtrum and nose. The moment Sean squinted her eyes open, wondering if she should—respond in kind?—the female abandoned her to inspect the mountain of beef on the sled. Dizziness rocked Sean so hard that she had to plant both hands on the ground, fully crouched and panting.

Then another warning growl leaked from the depths of the forest. Sean's breath stuttered at the familiar timbre. Her chest locked around an impossible wolfish noise; she physically couldn't respond in kind, even if she badly wanted to. Unable to help herself, she lifted her gaze from her submissive posture and caught eyes with her girl, her Kate—whose lips peeled snarling from her teeth at the presumption. Dried blood clung in a halo around her ruff, dotted her ears and snout, streaked across her flanks. She wore the cost of her survival, an armor of gore. Her siblings perked ears over their meals but didn't approach or intervene, as if curious to see their sister's response to a second intruder in one cycle. Sean bared her teeth once more, an invitation with bowed neck, and thought at her with every ferocious, enamored molecule: *you know me.*

But her partner-wolf, the one whose flesh and dreams she'd shared in communion, gave her a wide, suspicious berth as she paced around the opposite side of the sled. No recognition showed through her ice-chip eyes; only suffering mistrust. She snagged her own hank of beef from the bounty, favoring a foreleg with matted fur glued down around an open gash—and never once lifting her glowering stare from Sean's prone body.

The gulf of difference between them yawned. Sean whined in the most functional inquisitive register her human throat could produce. All three sets of ears tipped toward her, briefly, before Kate's bristling disregard prompted the others to ignore her as well. Stung by the rejection, Sean sat for another moment, listening with some cold comfort to her pack's snuffling, desperate consumption of the meal she'd offered. In their distraction, she hoped she'd be able to maneuver for the medical supplies—except the instant she crawled closer to the sled, Kate let out a bone-shuddering growl that brooked no misunderstanding. Sean froze stiff, then on no further response, inched her reaching arm down toward her lap once more. Kate tossed her head to swallow a hunk of beef, crouching mere feet from her—the closest they'd physically been since the cramped operating theater—but somehow, as distantly cool and unreachable as the sky overhead. The electric stitching between their heads counted for nothing; the conduit ran in only one direction. Shame sank Sean's stomach.

"Hey," she murmured to her girl, her wolf, flinging herself at the barrier of language between them. "I'm, uh, I'm sorry I left you alone."

Gold eyes searched her face, alien and overwhelming in their regard. Sean floated in a strange, uneasy state of capture. If the pack allowed her, she'd cart the medical supplies into the forest, locate their mother, and ply her with the best care she could offer—even if it was simply palliative. Patterns of posture and vocalization, which she understood loosely, indicated the sibling trio had not decided among themselves what to do with her. Bringing flesh to fill their bellies wasn't enough to garner an open welcome—the concept of gifts remained opaque, untranslated across their gulf. One last idea floated through Sean's memories, and before her courage gave up the ghost, she flopped backward onto the hard turf to bare her belly with limbs spread lax in imitation of a fellow wolf—just, wearing the wrong skin. *No threat.*

A pause, notable silence, before paw pads crunched grass in slow approach to her vulnerable head. Sean flicked her eyes sideways and saw Kate coming near—the de facto leader, now, she supposed. Her fingers curled into her palms. Up close, the remnant gore decorating her coat felt threatening and hyperreal. Her wolf paced a slow, considering circle around the open bowl of her body—dense claws passing inches from flesh under a thin layer of clothing. Without warning, Kate shoved her whole bony snout into the crook of Sean's armpit for a curious huff; she sank her teeth into her tongue to hold in a scream. The edges of her teeth pressed firm against Sean's rib bones, which had never felt so close to the surface of her skin before. Sean risked nudging a hand against her uninjured foreleg, stroking the backs of her knuckles across the muscle and tendon. Kate rumbled another deep growl, vibrating their chests in unison. Her wounded foreleg stepped across Sean's torso, a half-straddle, as their jawbones slid sidelong—then, at the precise moment of giddy horror where Sean considered the possibility of being eaten by her research subject, the wolf jerked to stiff attention above her.

Kate's lips skinned back off her teeth, her hackles rising as she stared alert across the length of the field toward the dirt road. Sean strained her ears, wheezing gently. The siblings rose to their feet as well, bloody-mawed, tense. Kate yipped and turned tail, her back leg catching against Sean's hip as she fled. The three wolves melted into the forest in a rush, disappearing as if they'd never been. Sean sat up, disoriented and adrenaline-sick. Phantom impressions of hot panting and solid teeth on her torso shivered like a lover's bite. Gathering herself took another long few minutes—waiting to see if the pack might return. When nothing else happened, she staggered to her feet and swung the medical supply bag over her shoulder. The tips of her ears had gone numb.

Finally, she heard the roar of an ATV.

"Shit, fuck," she grunted.

They'd found her sooner than she expected, by an order of magnitude, though she couldn't guess how long she'd spent pinned breathless under her wolf. Hobbling encumbered toward the forest, the trail marked in her mind's eye despite the encroaching night, she figured if she escaped from line of sight—

—but vehicles crossed terrain much faster than clumsy human feet.

"Doctor," an unfamiliar voice called out. The ATV puttered to an idle a few yards behind her. "Put the bag down, please."

Weighing the odds of what a colleague would be willing to do to stop her, she kept walking. She'd taken things this far already.

"Don't make me tranq you, because I absolutely will," they shouted.

"Fuck off," Sean shouted right back.

"I know you're trying to help, but you're not a vet, okay? Turn around and look at me," the interloper demanded.

Sean spun on her heel, nearly overbalanced with the weight of her supplies. The lamp from the ATV blinded her. She wobbled. The cold had leeched into her joints, everything from elbows to hips aching fiercely. She still had to make amends for the harm she'd done her pack, and she had no intention of stopping before she finished. She lifted an arm to protect against the accusatory glare and it shut off, leaving white sparklers across her ruined vision.

"Your team contacted me at the field station to make sure you weren't out here after your wife couldn't find you. I told them I doubted it, but lo and behold. You okay?" Dr. June said.

Sean dropped the supplies bag with a thud. Somewhere to her north the pack might be observing this exchange, the noise and stink of machinery. She was as trapped as her animal compatriot had been weeks ago: stiff as a board, freezing to the bone, pursuers far better equipped than she was. She had inflicted that trauma on Kate under the same aegis of taking *care* of her.

"I'm fine, but I'm not coming unless you agree to help Kate. She needs medical treatment," she croaked, clinging to the illusion of consent.

June said, "Yeah, the team told me why you'd gone AWOL. I've got Tom here with me and we're gonna go look after the injured as best we can, but you're going to stay the fuck here. You've already messed up your own research protocols bad enough, I don't need your help screwing mine."

If she wanted to be near a wolf, there were plenty of rescue and captive subjects to engage with across the globe—but those wolves weren't *hers*, and she wasn't theirs either. Braced against her own fight-or-flight response, she blinked through the dazzle of her returning vision to squint at the doctor's face.

"Promise me you'll help her," Sean said. Her shivering intensified.

"We'll do what we can for them, so long as you're not going to tattle on us for messing with your pristine subjects," the research assistant said.

Sean winced. With that rhetorical blow struck, she allowed herself to be gathered into chafing hands and her clothes stuffed with heat packs. The ATV seat radiated warmth to her thighs and butt as she collapsed onto it. Lingering rotten-meat spit in her mouth was all that remained of her brief encounter with her pack and the handsome she-wolf who saw her as a stranger.

EEG pads bristled from Sean's skull like porcupine quills, the netting webbed from her cheekbones over her forehead and around to the base of her spine. The lab's dull yellow-tinged comfort lighting cast shadows beneath the furniture and equipment, creating an unsettling topography. A digital clock on the wall informed her that it was past 3 p.m., which meant the testing battery had lasted a full six hours. Hours of fMRI mapping left Sean hyperaware of her skeleton. Though she knew she had no metal implants, while lying corpse-still in the clanking, thunking, howling machine she had imagined the magnetic force pulling her pelvis and shoulder sockets crooked.

"We're about to begin," Aseem said, voice worn thin.

"Fire away," Sean grumbled.

The Chilson-Reed implant behind her temple steadily radiated pain. Migraines and lingering dread had kept her up through the night, even after Riya dropped off to sleep holding her. The evening before, Aseem had arrived to the field site with her wife in tow, bearing more hot packs to restore her extremities to a reasonable temperature—but her guts were still frozen. While Aseem exchanged quiet conversation with Dr. June, Riya laid her hand on the crown of Sean's head and said nothing. She felt like a misbehaving child who'd run away from home. The sled of perishables and medical supplies sat near their sad little huddle, accusatory and mad. Her attempt to approach her pack, her partner-wolf, had been a grand misfire. As Riya nudged her to standing off the ATV, June's walkie-talkie crackled then piped through her assistant's voice: *located the mature female, but we're too late. I'm sorry.* The mother's bones would remain where she lay in her final moments, at the root of a broad old tree. Unburied—food for other starving scavengers. The circle of fucking life.

Sean forced a long sigh out of her nose, resisting the urge to scratch her face under the electrodes: researcher turned subject. While Aseem and Alex took turns guiding her through a set of focus exercises, she tried not to let her mind wander to their corporate overlords. Per the funding terms, the team had been feeding Chilson-Reed biweekly updates from the official field notes alongside the mountain of raw data. Anything within the team's cloud server was accessible to their bankrollers for the purpose of assessing progress, despite the company's lack of experience in her field of research.

Sean had received confirmation that, despite the fantasies she'd built upon those spikes in the neural feed, no automatic connection had been established between her and Kate. Without the interface, she remained a foreign creature to her wolf, not a ghost in the machine Kate could recognize as one of her own family. In the cold daylight of a medical lab, even sidelong acknowledgement of the belief she'd been nursing humiliated her—the entire dream, the hope, so terribly *woo-woo*. A mechanical circuit couldn't flip itself closed. Her intimacies were all as one-sided as people said, and that truth stung worse than the persistent stabbing inside her skull. At some point, she needed to clean up the mess of her mistaken assumptions and spin her sudden change of heart—which had almost certainly fucked up their experiment beyond repair—to her venture capital masters.

"All done," Alex said as he reentered the room. His falsely chipper demeanor grated on Sean's nerves.

"Will I be allowed to review the scans, or is the mutiny complete?" Sean asked.

"You're still the boss," Alex said. His laugh was strained, his hands careful as he stripped off the sensors one at a time. The residual adhesive itched. "You just weren't super yourself yesterday, and I totally get why. It sucks, and it was awkward for us too, but it is what it is."

"Apologies," she managed, unconvincingly.

"We've worked together how long? You know I respect you," Alex murmured.

None of them had brought up her going off the rails the night before, nothing whatsoever about it being her personal reenactment of *Julie of the Wolves*. The elision made her want to shout, but instead, she let the conversation fizzle and pried herself off the padded recliner. No more tests left. Riya had offered to cancel her seminar for the afternoon, but Sean assured her it was unnecessary since she planned to come home right afterward. The crimped frown she received in response flashed through her memories like a dull-edged knife, scraping open the top layer of her skin. Riya hadn't asked her what the fuck she'd thought she was doing either. Aseem leaned over the imaging monitor with the technician, pointing to the screen. His concerned grimace was—foreboding.

First he asked, "How's your head?"

"Hurts like a bastard," she said.

"Do you need a break or shall we return to the lab to review?"

"I'm good to work," she said.

Labor would distract her from her worries for the pack, the project, and their data problems. Though the field biologists had removed the supplies and sundries she'd hauled out to the field, she knew—having watched them give each other raised-eyebrow glances and conspicuously leave the meat behind—that neither of them fully disagreed with her failed attempt to offer aid. Her team, on the other hand, she couldn't be sure of.

"Please send these all over to us," Aseem said with a pat on the technician's shoulder.

"I'm going to grab a coffee on the walk back, I'll meet you there," Sean said.

The pair of men keeping an eye on her, as if their hovering was even remotely surreptitious, nodded in agreement. She yanked her winter coat on, toggled the buttons closed at the middle and throat, and left the imaging lab alone for the first time in eighteen hours. Her bursting, out-of-control emotions frustrated her, an impediment to the work that needed to be done. Rationality hovered at a remove while she snapped at Alex, glowered at Aseem, and nursed an insulted rage at the lot of them for not responding to the wolves' pain as she did. Or, maybe she was just punishing them for seeing her lose her shit, be fallible and vulnerable. If she wanted another session with her wolf, once Christian's reportage finished, she needed to perform some measure of objectivity. And to do that, she'd have to concoct a justification for offering support to the pack. She could claim she'd gone a little rogue, maybe trying to kick-start some interspecies cooperation on her own.

The moneymen wouldn't risk their reputation on a clumsy project that failed due to emotionality—not from a woman researcher. The optics were terrible. She cringed internally, ordering her mocha with two extra shots at the campus Starbucks. Maybe if Riya had been at home, or her team had been willing to communicate with her, she wouldn't have flung herself at the one creature she felt she could be intimate with, as false as that feeling might be. While she waited for the coffee, her phone buzzed. She tapped open the text from Aseem, which read, *come to lab asap.*

A chill pricked at her neck. She booked it back to the lab without getting her coffee, and entering the room, saw Christian standing with one arm hugging their own waist and the other palm pressed over the lower half of their face. On the projection screen, sketchy waveforms plastered alongside colorful resonance imaging butted up against simple gray scans. Aseem sat ramrod straight in his chair, typing furiously. His phone lay on the desk at his elbow. Dahye's and Alex's backs were to them at their own workstations, raw interface data streaming across their screens.

Sean halted in place. "What's wrong?"

Christian tapped their fingers on their cheekbone in agitation, glancing at her then at the screen again. "Come look at this and tell me what you're seeing."

Their technical skill set differed from the rest of the team's, smashing a hodgepodge of field expertises into a broadly applicable set of problem-solving skills. Sean trusted their eye, if nothing else. Her empty stomach sank as she traced over the rows of images forward then backward, over and over again to be sure of what she was seeing.

"The bottom row has significant alterations in activity patterns and also . . . also physical structure compared to the preceding rows," she said. Christian nodded. Sean hugged her own elbows. "Those are from this afternoon, aren't they? Those are me."

"The first is from before your implant, the second is after the test treatment weeks, the third is current," Aseem confirmed.

"That's not supposed to happen," Sean said.

"No, it's very much not," Christian replied tersely.

"We have to report this to Chilson-Reed," Aseem said.

Sean approached the screens, inspecting her own brain as dispassionately as possible. The experiment's length was negligible in the span of her life—but it had changed her chemical being, altered the fatty whorls inside her skull. She put both hands on the desk and dropped her head. Trying to dive into another being without giving anything of herself in return had been an act of real arrogance, but the wolf had found a way to get inside her regardless.

"I don't feel different," she eventually said, blank with realization.

"I need to reach out to the dev team and our VP, and like, every other person I can think of to see if there's a record of that sort of damage from the initial trials," Christian said.

"It's unclear if the change is harmful," Sean corrected. Their panicked tone could take away her last chance to give her wolf a goodbye, a final intercourse of minds—after all, the damage was already done. "Maybe it's something else, an evolution. We could've guessed that entanglement would produce unexpected effects."

Christian gave her an incredulous look. "I'm as culpable as anyone, but you do realize the reason this got venture funding *from my company* is that no sane federal body would've let you use yourself as a human subject, right?"

"And who knows what being hooked onto your brain has done to the wolf in turn," Aseem muttered.

"We're pretty sure the answer is nothing good," Dahye said reluctantly from behind them.

Sean turned on her heel. Dahye's chagrined expression spoke clearly. The spiking, oscillating data on her screen looped through the same minute of recording over and over, a wild scribble of colors that scrawled from almost the top of the graph to the bottom. The spacious room squeezed close. Alex scrolled backward to play a longer selection of the recordings, where once again her wolf's normal range of neural activities abruptly exploded with disorganized, scribbling feedback.

"That's when the interface activated the last time. I'm figuring each time we turned it on, the reverberations got worse; negligible at first, but . . ." he said.

"If we stop using the interface"—Sean paused to swallow sick-spit at the thought of being cut loose too soon—"will the spikes stop?"

"I don't know. Would it matter, at this point, is the other question," Dahye said with a resolute sort of sadness.

Sean's lingering worries over the cold season and the bear attack, the pack's food supply and group cohesion, washed out on the tide of a larger and guiltier terror: that *she* had caused Kate grievous harm. Worse than all of those other threats combined, by an order of magnitude—while glorying in the intimacies she swallowed whole. She said, "I need to step outside for a minute."

Hurrying from the lab, Sean passed Christian tapping furiously on their phone with pinched-taut brow and lifted shoulders. She recalled the PR puff piece about recreational opportunities to be gleaned from her conservation work. Failure of the experiment to produce significant data was one thing, but the collapse of the project around health and safety concerns was another realm of fucked up entirely. The ball of catastrophe kept on rolling downhill, picking up speed as it went. Ass planted on the wall and bent double, elbows on her knees, Sean drew in gut-deep breaths. The C. R. implant inside her skull sat neutral, inactive, but she pictured it as a ticking bomb. The door swung open a moment later. Aseem sat on the floor beside her. She glanced at his bowed head. Two curious strangers strolled past, crossing from their own workrooms to the toilets.

He said, "I'm so very sorry."

"What happens next?" she asked, though she didn't genuinely want to know.

Aseem dropped his head back against the wall, met her down-turned gaze, and shook his head. They sat together, silent, listening to the faint murmur of Christian's anxious phone call drifting from underneath the lab door.

After being fed home-baked bread and a rich vegetable stew, Sean lay soaking in the oil-shimmering bath Riya had run for her. The last forty-eight hours weighed her down like a mountain of sand, crumbling in her eyes and mouth, grinding between her bones in their sockets. Steaming water eased some of the physical aches, but the psychic wounds cut deeper. Through the cracked bathroom door, Sean watched Riya move around the bedroom—changing into her silk pajamas, turning the end-table lamp on and the overheads off. At a quarter past nine she heaved herself out of the bath and dried the slick dampness from her skin, chapped red in patches from her outing.

When she emerged nude in search of pajamas, Riya glanced up from the book she was pretending to read in bed. Her gaze skittered loose from her partner's nakedness until Sean finished dressing and slid under the covers, lying flat on her back to blink at the ceiling. Riya reached out to click the lamp off, and in the following dark, ran her thumb along the line of Sean's jaw to her earlobe. When Sean sighed, she switched to her index finger and traced the delicate shell, bumping across the scar of an old helix piercing. Grasping the short length of hair on the side of her head, she tilted Sean's head on the pillow. Their eyes met. "What did all those tests tell you?" she asked.

That I restructured my brain, and I don't know what that means for me or Kate or the experiment. Out loud, she said, "We're not totally sure. Christian is reaching out to Chilson-Reed and I expect we'll have some of their experts on hand tomorrow."

"Aseem told me what happened to your wolves on the drive out to get you. I understand feeling like you had to—help them, somehow . . . and I'm so sorry you lost one. I really mean that," she said.

"It sucks," Sean admitted in a whisper.

Dampness clogged her eyes. She blinked it loose, one drop rolling across the bridge of her nose to fall to the pillow. Riya crooned and wiped the trailing moisture with the blade of her palm. Her prominent collarbone stood in relief against the sea-green of her sleeping top. Beneath the covers she wore briefs and nothing else. Sean remembered almost a decade of nights spent in bed opposite one another, animated by greedy hands and good intentions—to the point where those pajamas had become a Pavlovian trigger for her arousal. But tonight her body ached too much; her heart ached too much. She had made all the wrong choices.

"Where were you last night when I texted?" Sean asked.

The corners of Riya's mouth flinched perceptibly. She said, "With a colleague, I was out for drinks that ran late."

Sean chose her words cautiously, asking, "Was it . . . the same colleague you were out with after the memorial service?"

Riya dropped her chin. Tension flowed from her, a decision made. She laid her hand across Sean's throat and collarbone, thumb pressed to her pulse. The steady thump stayed even despite the exhausted sorrow dragging her limbs into a relaxed sprawl across the mattress.

"Yes," she admitted.

"You don't have to say it, I already *know*," Sean said.

Riya sighed and scooted close to push their foreheads together, near enough that Sean's eyes crossed and she closed them. Minty toothpaste breath tickled her nostrils. The straight dense curtain of Riya's hair drifted across her pillow and chin. Another illusion: a physical intimacy, without being able to see into one another's hearts for what was, or wasn't, there.

"How many times did you—did it happen?" Sean asked.

"I swear, only three times. The first after the memorial, then that weekend I was gone, and also . . . last night." Riya's voice dropped to a whisper. "While you were alone, out there."

The strange amalgamation of closeness and separation, listening to her wife's confession behind the still darkness of her eyelids, made it easier to process. While the sibling wolf had been licking into her mouth in greeting, her wife might've been licking across another woman's chest; at the moment she'd offered Kate her belly, let her stand over top of her, had Riya been seated astride a stranger's face with knees pinning her hair? She pictured the other woman inverse of herself: sporting a luscious mane and graspable plump curves, giving and accessible, the kind of temptation that she could see herself slipping for. Maybe the sex had been serviceable and boring, a way to scratch an itch, or maybe it had been phenomenal. She wasn't as bothered as she expected to be. "Do you want to know who it was, will that help?" Riya asked.

"I don't think so," Sean said.

"Okay. It wasn't even good, it was just . . . I did it but I'm not sure why," she said.

"It's fine if it was good," Sean muttered, her eyes still shut.

"But it wasn't," she insisted. Her small shudder ground their foreheads together.

Riya's breath hitched, like she was about to start crying. Sean wrapped both arms around her midriff and hugged hard, crushing her wife against her chest. Riya wheezed, back popping, but she clutched her in return. Shipwrecked on the life raft of their bed and dragging each other under the current, Sean huffed the scent of her wife's hair for comfort. Neither of them said *sorry*.

"Go fuck yourself," Sean snarled at the conference-call panel of three white men in designer suits—three varying shades of charcoal—projected on the main screen, floating above the team.

The man whose video cube sat farthest to the left, his salt-and-pepper beard neatly trimmed, grimaced minutely. Christian buried their face in their hands. Sean glowered at the screen. Her mood was already foul from another night spent watching her wife snore gently while lancing beats of migraine kept jerking her out of dreamless, wispy shreds of sleep. She thought she'd have more time to create a game plan to deal with Chilson-Reed, but the higher-ups had demanded an immediate conference.

Middle-cube guy, who looked young enough to be her kid in an-other universe, said, "I understand you're upset, but you applied for our grant *and* signed our contracts agreeing to the terms of funding, including IP rights."

"The results our teammate sent over are of deep concern to the whole development team, Dr. Kell-Luddon," the last man said, de-void of expression and seated in front of a tinted-glass wall with a sweeping vista over the San Francisco Bay. "The interface is never supposed to alter structures in the brain, just provide more targeted chemical assistance than the average prescription pill can manage. Your test results are a clear reason to exercise . . . caution, going for-ward."

"*Exercising caution* does not tell me why you're revoking our fund-ing or demanding to seize our materials," Aseem pointed out as Sean seethed. *Materials* of course included their documents, data, and tech—but also served as a neat euphemism for their nonhuman research subject, her living wolf. The youngest opened his mouth again, but Aseem continued, "Our team is perfectly well-equipped to continue to research the causes of the anomaly; if you'll simply allow us to adapt the scope—"

Salt-and-pepper cut him off. "We'd prefer to do that research in-house. Frankly, our concern is twofold: one, the safety reputation of our product, and two, the study of potential side effects that would help us develop future initiatives. It's outside of your parameters. And *our* teams cannot do that important labor without collecting the subject for thorough examination."

"You mean killing her to see what happened to her brain," Sean said.

"It's regrettable, but you understand it's how these things go," he responded with a sardonic eyebrow. "You're a scientist as much as I am, Doctor. You should understand that the cost of progress is painful to extract. I'm surprised at the vehemence of your response. I'm aware you're . . . quite attached to this subject, but the animal is no different from the thousand and one mice your lab must've gone through this year. It's a hard call to make, but the information we're able to gather will have real value."

"Gray wolves are endangered. You can't just kill her," Sean said—hating the desperate tinge of her voice.

Stone-faced guy, the legal representative, slicked a weird smile over his thin mouth. Maybe telling them to get fucked had peeved him. Sean figured that wasn't how they were used to being spoken to. The baby dev lead's insouciant slouch belied the concern in his little sympathetic grimace.

Legal guy said, "I think you'll find that we can. Collecting the subject is within our rights, as our hardware is in her body and the approval from the ethics committee clearly stated the lethal potential of the study. There's no way to collect it without damaging her, just as you drew out in your project proposal. High risk, high reward. We need to determine what effects the broadcasting neural netting has on a subject."

"Then you might as well collect the brain out of me too," Sean snapped.

The science head said, "I'm surprised to hear such lack of perspective from our lead researcher, though given your tantrum about the PR piece, maybe I shouldn't be. Regardless, you and your team will be compensated for any patents that employ your collected data. We might be able to salvage some of the more positive experiences you recorded for public access VR. Boost morale, encourage conservation, and whatnot."

Stealing isolated pieces from the life they intended to destroy then packaging them for sale. Sean reached across the gap between her sullen, shocked team and the keyboard to smack the exit key twice, cutting off the video call. Christian snorted. Aseem winced but did not contradict her.

"Holy shit," Alex said.

"I can't do anything about this. It's completely out of my hands," Christian said.

"Yeah, you're just an attaché," Sean snapped, not concerned with professional courtesy.

"I'll have the uni lawyers take a look, Sean, but I suspect they know their fine print. We agreed to their terms," Aseem said.

She stood from her chair, resisting the urge to kick it across the room, and hissed, "Private *fucking* capital."

"The results aren't good for corporate PR," Dahye said, "so they're scrapping the whole thing, gagging us on the results, and destroying the evidence."

"It looks bad if their magic machine scrambles people's brains, huh," Alex replied.

"Yes, it does," Christian agreed. Without looking at Sean they ventured, "But—and I'm not trying to make excuses here, honestly—if we're more mad about them collecting our subject than about them cutting us off from the research, it isn't like our original proposal was much different. Putting the mesh in might've killed Kate, using the interface might've killed her and did damage her, observing her through the winter was implicitly allowing her to die while we gathered data. It does seem hypocritical to set the life of an individual wolf as our moral event horizon."

The team sat in silence. Sean paced from one end of the lab to the other. Her sneakers squeaked on the tile each time she turned, burning off furious energy while her headache pounded onward. If Chilson-Reed intended to muzzle her and kill her counterpart, maybe she'd sue them for giving her brain damage—except she knew without looking that particular ass would be covered by the contracts. She had treated the wolf as an object from the start, until she got wrapped up inside her as a real being. That was on her. Kate hadn't ever had a choice in participating, and she wouldn't get a choice now in how her memories would be reproduced for consumption—all those intimate shared affects Sean had scribbled in her journals, dissected for sale.

"But it's not fair, it's not her *fault*," she burst out.

Aseem said, "Given that she's been devolving, perhaps this is a kindness to her. She won't have to live with the degenerative effects that seem very likely, if we extrapolate from her current state. The damage is done."

"How is it a kindness to murder her?" Sean demanded, whirling on him as she suffocated in a cloud of her own hubris.

"She's not a person, my friend," he reminded. Compassion showed in his reticent folded arms, his pressed-together knees. "And Christian is correct that we've done this to her, each of us. If Chilson-Reed intends to pursue this avenue regardless, wouldn't you rather see her through to the end?"

"If we ask them to let us participate, at least we can say goodbye," Dahye said.

"Jesus Christ, I have to get out of here," Sean choked out through a closing throat. Her wild eyes caught on the short stack of journals and she grabbed them. "None of you tell them about these. I'm not handing them over, you hear me?"

No one followed her outside to the blistering chill, sans coat and gloves. The unforgiving winter sun glared high overhead, light reflected off the sheen of ice covering dips in the sidewalks, dirty salt and slush underfoot. It was supposed to have been simple and grand: *haven't you always wanted to know how it feels to be a wolf?* But now, the loss of two strong hunting bodies over the span of one week might doom the pack. The adolescent would have two fewer tongues to clean his face, two fewer warm bodies to curl against through the night. And also—also, Sean wouldn't ever smell the forest through her wolf's nose again, wouldn't share in her pleasures or pains as she lay with her siblings, loped through a cold stream, cracked the bones of a squirrel between her jaws. The colors she saw for the first time, saturated and green-tinged and strange, weren't hers any longer. Sean was even more alone than before. She sat on the frozen dead-grass berm, ignoring the water soaking into the seat of her pants, and sobbed into crossed arms.

The email she'd received lying in her bed alone at five in the afternoon—having left the lab without a goodbye, following her breakdown—informed her that Chilson-Reed would proceed with their plans to collect their property the following evening. As a gesture of good faith, her team would be allowed to watch the proceedings, though no further participation in their research or access to their data would be allowed. The last two pages of the email contained brutalist fine-print reminders of various NDAs and her legal exposure if she chose to go public. When Riya got home she found Sean curled up on the dog-bed with Miller, weeping again. She didn't ask, simply ran a hand over her hair and whispered, "I'll make some dinner."

She returned to the lab in funeral blacks, with a white starched tie, at a quarter past six the next evening. Hothouse wildflowers scattered the main worktop in a miserable approximation of grieving bouquets. Her whole team—soon to be strangers to her again, unless she found another project to recruit them to after the grant dissolved—were gathered in waiting for her, the livestream pulled up. Sean settled into her office chair with a muttered greeting, gripping the chair arms white-knuckled. The muscles in her jaw crunched as she cranked her mouth wide to soothe the cramping. Gloomy silence settled as the team stared at the video feed of the vacant veterinary surgery theater.

The alert had come forty-five minutes earlier. Chilson-Reed's field technicians had located Kate, tranquilized her, and removed her for transport. No other members of the pack had been harmed in the process. On the trap-cameras, the black containment box in the bed of the truck had loomed waiting until her limp body was bundled into it. Over the transmission, Kate seemed scrawny in the hunters' arms—not the muscled, lean creature who frolicked and adored her siblings and cared for her youngest as if he was her own whelp. No larger than a big helpless dog who deserved better than she got.

"I negotiated reading access to their results after the autopsy, under the terms that we need to be able to manicure our publication around their nondisclosure requirements. We can confirm whether or not she'd have survived with the neural mesh for much longer, regardless of this," Aseem said.

"Cold fucking comfort, man," Sean replied.

"We knew the season might end with the loss of our subject, or the whole pack," Alex reminded her.

Sean shook her head, attention locked on the screen. To Alex and Dahye and Aseem and Christian alike, no matter their empathetic response to her obvious pain, this was a work-related failure. Irritating because it meant dispersing to other research positions, losing the opportunity to publish their full set of data, and perhaps a little sad by virtue of having bonded with the image of the wolf pack. Depressing, but in the same way reading news stories about habitat destruction and climate refugees and *are we citizens of an oligarchy* was depressing. The pain was out there somewhere, but impersonal— nothing for them to repent about, get eaten up inside over.

The gurney rolled beneath the camera's lens in the hands of two animal surgeons, neither of whom Sean recognized. The brindled wolf's chest rose and fell in shallow heaves. The siblings would be missing her again, worried over her disappearance and the intrusive scents tracked all over her last known location. Unlike the last

time, she wouldn't be coming home. Sean imagined them waiting—
hoping less and less as the weeks dragged on. The oldest male had
lost his mate and his adult child at once. Sean had taken that from
him, from the whole pack. Pouring the suffering of Kate's passing
into her eyes was what she deserved.

One surgeon prepared the set of syringes. Sean chewed the sides of
her tongue until she tasted blood. Her first encounter with Kate had
been in a mobile operating theater, and her last would be too. Sean
had chosen all their intimacies, never putting them on equal footing.

Dahye said, "The interface is still recording her output. It will
until the end."

A collective shiver went through the team: a final output from her
sleeping mind, struggling as the drugs took hold. The surgeon ad-
dressed the camera, informing them of the procedure in a monotone
voice—first an additional sedative, then the euthanasia injections,
then an autopsy. Sean watched the needle glide into the vein on
Kate's unwounded foreleg. The nasty gash the bear left on the other
leg would never heal. It had all happened so fast. The second needle went in smoothly too, but watching her wolf's handsome body
begin to shake with minuscule convulsions broke Sean's resolve and
brought her gorge rising fast. She stumbled out of her chair, tripped
over Dahye's legs, and crashed through the door to the hallway. Two
steps later, she vomited. Another employee yelped and jumped for
the hall phone to call maintenance, while a second bystander asked
if she was all right. Sean waved them off to let her stagger for the
bathroom. She rinsed her mouth, washed her face.

The dull horror on her face under the bad, hard lighting made her
look like a corpse. Writing another grant, building another team,
digging her fingers into some other living creature's guts—crawling
back to Chilson-Reed or another corporate board just like theirs—
she wouldn't do it. And if she wasn't going to do that, then she
didn't belong in the niche she'd spent her whole life carving out,
fighting to be the best and brightest and most innovative researcher
she knew. The *rock star*. Riya was right about her.

In a haze, she walked back to the lab and stood in the doorframe.
The muted, visceral sounds of wet work came from the speakers,
though she couldn't see the screen. She traced the blank expressions
of her team and said, into their miserable faces, "I quit."

"What?" Aseem jolted in his chair, turning to look at her.

"I said, I quit," Sean repeated—hearing herself echoing from a distance. "Send me a draft of whatever they allow you to write, I don't care if I'm named on the paper or not. I'm done."

Without listening to their clamor of responses, she floated across the room, scooped her laptop into her bag with her keys, and took one glance at the gruesome tableaux on-screen overhead. Her stomach churned, acidic. No product that came from the bloody dissection of her bond with Kate deserved to be published, but it would be; she wondered how long Chilson-Reed would wait before they made good on their virtual reality plan. Alex hushed the group as she paused in the doorframe, looking across their faces one more time and feeling nothing.

On the trip home she stopped in the liquor store to snag a bottle of scotch. Riya was reading on the couch when she crossed through the main hall to the kitchen. She followed Sean in a moment later and watched her pour a full old-fashioned glass of liquor over ice, no chaser. Sean couldn't bear to be seen in mourning, so she said, "I'll talk about it tomorrow," and locked herself in their shared office for the night.

Sean stuffed four appointments with her therapist into the barren expanse of the next two weeks, otherwise spent pacing the house in sweatpants and taking long naps through the afternoons, chasing the simple desire to be *still*. Throughout the trough of her grief, Riya treated her with the kind compassion of a roommate. Sean drank too much; she refused to shower; she dodged emails and phone calls from the human resources department and her department chair and the provost; she dreamed about a surgeon's hands in her dead guts. The world continued on around her. One morning she came downstairs to see a stack of application materials for another overseas job posting, covered in red ink—Riya's tall scrawling letters splashed all over the pages. Her wife hadn't shown up smelling of strangers' perfume again while she drifted around their house like flotsam, one small blessing.

On the first morning of the third week Sean sat at the table with her laptop at full charge and her contact lenses in, wearing a pair of actual jeans. Her therapist had suggested creating a list of alternate careers. He'd also told her to sit down with her wife for a real talk about the future. Instead of doing either of those things, she opened her university email and skimmed the stacked-up correspondence. Junk mail, lab reports, and campus updates she shunted aside. She opened several red-flagged HR emails to find offers of compassionate leave and requests for her to a call them immediately to plan her lab's dispensations. She sighed from the depths of her belly and began tapping out responses, informing the powers-that-be of her commitment to resignation.

Last on the docket was a personal email with an attachment that read,

Dear Sean,

   I hope you're well. Perhaps when the fog has passed over us all, we can go for drinks. I miss your company around the office. I won't ask if you intend on returning anytime soon, but know you'd be welcome at our home anytime if you need a friend to talk to. I've attached the article draft we compiled out of the data C. R. allowed us to publish; I've taken the liberty of including your name, as you spearheaded our work, but have tried not to put words in your mouth.

Be well,

Aseem

She opened the document. Chilson-Reed had laid claim to all data relating to the neural interface, in effect creating a gag order covering the results and implications of her portion of the project. The administration's lawyers hadn't been interested in fighting the capital juggernaut for the sake of one underfunded research team. The conservation-oriented field observations of the pack still belonged to Sean's team, but none of the affective or sensorium data was available for them to reproduce.

The abstract twaddled on about the parameters of the project's concern with interspecies relationality, arguing that *based on documented observation, cooperative behaviors are reliant on and produced through the actions of singular individuals within the structural unit and are then reproduced through consensus behavior.* Sean skimmed forward to the results and found a clinical description of the pack's conflict with the bear based on her field notes. Without the emotions in her journals, the reportage was barren. Her wolf's fear and pain at the loss of her mother, her anxieties over the encroaching terror of the lean cold months, were absent.

They'd summed up actions and left all the *feeling* out. The paper made Kate into another generic wolf to be destroyed for human consumption. She flipped to the end and found no mention of the grim end of her wolf's life. It was astounding all over again, seeing the lack of accountability made concrete. She'd bought a pathetic blip of a publication with Kate's life, a paper she doubted would get more than a handful of citations. Disgusted and tired, she slapped the laptop shut. Her pack deserved better than she'd given them by far.

Riya was due home in another short while. For the sake of doing something with her hands before she lost it, Sean set to work shredding kale for an apple-pistachio-Craisin salad. The damp, cool greens tore between her fingers with satisfactory resistance. She twisted them into ever-finer component parts, tossing each destroyed fistful into the salad bowl. The front door opened and Miller began his usual welcoming cacophony, just as she was drizzling lemon-balsamic vinaigrette over the greens.

"In the kitchen," she announced.

Riya padded in barefoot a moment later, tucking the ends of her long skirt through the waistband to kilt it up. A messy bun narrowly contained her silver-glossed dark hair. While she set the table, making small talk about her seminar, Sean fried up a pair of eggs. The popping of butter and the rich, faintly smoky smell of the edges crisping filled the air.

"I turned in my resignation," Sean said to the stovetop, flipping the final egg.

Riya dragged a chair out and sat, letting the statement settle, before she responded, "And how does that feel?"

Plates in hand, Sean sat across from her. She looked at the sunspots and fine wrinkles on the backs of her own hands, the wedding band. "Honestly, it doesn't feel like anything. But the thought of going into that lab again and proposing another project like that one, working with the same people who couldn't see how *fucked up* what happened was—I couldn't. I can't."

Riya nodded. Sean chewed a bite of greens, stomach panging with a dissatisfied craving for meat. *Aseem sent me the draft*, she considered admitting. *It made me feel like shit, and I'm going to have nightmares about the bear again after reading it, sorry.* But before she managed, Riya said, "I got together some documents I thought you'd maybe be willing to look over?"

Sean swallowed. "Legal ones?"

Riya startled in her seat before wincing apologetically. "No, god, sorry. But since you'd been leaning toward quitting I thought I'd help . . . brainstorm where you'd like to go next? Hang on, I'll be back."

She stood before Sean could agree. Her quick steps tapped on the hardwood into the front hall and back. She dropped a multicolor-highlighted sheaf of pages between them. Her brow was pinched with an embarrassed but determined look. Sean snagged the stack and slid it toward herself, reading from the header, CONSERVATION NONPROFITS & MUTUAL AID ORGANIZATIONS. Skimming through the orgs on the first page, stomach doing flips, she saw several address listings in or, she presumed, *around* Delhi.

"I'm suggesting that . . ." Riya trailed off, and cleared her throat. "Okay, I don't want to make you a proposal. But after what happened last month, this is the most change I've ever seen in you, and I thought maybe . . ."

The cautiously warm hope in her partner's tone, compared to the stilted circling they'd been doing since her injury, made her sinuses burn with emotion.

"Come on, spit it out," Sean said.

Riya huffed. "I think you learned something, and I should give that a chance, yeah? So, if you're seriously thinking about changing your line of work, or of giving back, all of that, then—why not find a place where I could meet you in the middle?"

"Why not," she echoed in a whisper.

Riya reached out and covered her hand on the printout, grip sturdy. Sean turned her palm so their fingers locked together. High-lighted names and descriptions of postings, some paid and some unpaid, swam across one another. She counted three separate wildlife rehabilitation centers. None of the places her wife offered her needed a disgraced neuroscientist; none of them required her to be in charge, or to use her expertise. She'd be able to fade into the background and practice penance, which might be better than moping around the house like a ghost, like she was the one who'd died. But she hadn't asked to be given a platter to choose from, like her future was one of the recipes hung on the fridge.

"Thanks," she said gracelessly. "I'll read them over. I don't know if I've decided what I'll do though, you know that?"

"Of course," Riya responded quickly. "That's all I'm asking, for you to consider starting fresh, somewhere else, with me."

"I'm just—a fucking wreck about it all still, Riya," Sean burst out. She pulled her hand back to cover her face and scrub the tension in her jaw with both thumbs. "I'm sorry. Give me some time."

An odd look crossed her wife's face at the word *time*. After the better part of a decade cataloguing her microexpressions, that one pinged her spine to straighten. She glanced at the list of job postings curated for her with care. Deliberately, she set her fork aside and began to riffle through the stack of sheets again—collated and organized by type of labor and in respect of her potential visa status. The implications weren't particularly subtle.

Over the top of the stack, she said, "You got the position."

"I did," Riya said.

"And did you accept?" she asked.

"I told them I'd respond tomorrow morning, but I intend to agree," she said.

The alien politeness of the exchange dug under Sean's skin. *Miller is too old to manage long travel and a pet quarantine,* she thought, watching him trot past blissfully unaware. Riya's fork plinked against her plate as she abandoned the pretense of eating, her salad barely dented. Sean tipped her head back to stare at the ceiling and process the rapid-fire blows of the past several weeks. Of course Riya should accept the position—the question was whether or not her freshly jobless wife would prefer to emigrate with her, learn more than thirty words in her parent language, make regular visits to her parents, and get into public service work she could be proud of. Those were the implicit parameters she'd sketched.

"Just one thing on top of another, isn't it," she said to herself.

"Hey, don't forget you got us here under your own steam," Riya said. "I told my mother that I'd be coming home soon. She asked after you, you know."

Sean rolled her chin to meet her eyes again, feeling their thawing softness. She just wasn't sure she had it in her to be a dependent.

"What would we do with Miller, or the house?" she asked.

"We'd figure it out if you wanted to. I'm not offering you blanket forgiveness, but like I said, you're changing—this is one last shot to see if it sticks, if the future you works with the future me," Riya said.

"I understand." Sean nudged at the salad and uneaten egg. "This sucks. Let's order pasta."

An hour later found them eating fettucine on the couch with their dog asleep between them, watching a documentary about bicycles. Sean made observations about butches on bikes; Riya pressed chilly toes to her thigh. The hollow beneath her gut remained unmoved. She performed the motions of companionship until Riya kissed her good night and left her sitting alone with the murmuring television—giving her room to think. Sean flicked channels for a while before giving in to the restless itch under her skin and moving to the study.

The last quarter of a bottle of scotch sat on her desk among the detritus of her dead project. Her journals, technically stolen and illicit research material, sat in a haphazard stack on the floor. She locked the door, pouring the dregs into her unwashed cup. She took a peaty sip. Offering her labor to a conservation group sounded logical, but her heart wasn't compelled. Instead, she opened her laptop and logged in through the burner VPN account she'd opened for the team when she began the project—miraculously, no one had shut the whole thing off—to locate the field station's camera feeds.

Along a familiar tree line, snow clung in fat sloping drifts to the earth. While she waited to catch a surreptitious glimpse of survivors, the packmates who hadn't paid with their bodies to feed the engine of progress, she checked her phone. An unfamiliar address stood out to her, time-stamped an hour before, with the subject line *Trade Publishing Inquiry*. The first flutter of curiosity buoyed up her insides. The message began,

To Dr. Kell-Luddon,

Following an off-record communication with a personal friend of mine with whom you've recently been working, I'm reaching out to inquire about your interest in pursuing a trade nonfiction project on your experiences with the last wild wolf pack. I'm given to understand that a nondisclosure agreement precludes certain aspects of academic publication, and you would be unable to expose specific practices or outcomes, but I would be pleased to see a pitch for a memoir or similar book based on your research. Our team would be able to assist you in navigating those legal requirements. My associate provided me with such compelling detail on the labor you undertook to bond with your particular wolf, and the deep emotional connection with nature that you experienced. Yours is the sort of story audiences are primed for right now. While it isn't the project you initially envisioned, I'd be interested in hearing from you, if you had a desire to immortalize your experience with your wolf in another form.

Best,
John Malcom

The flutter resolved into a warm, writhing tug of intrigue. She'd have to be careful to avoid discussing the research parameters or the technical aspects, the funding or the project dissolution, but the nondisclosure couldn't entirely silence her experience of the world she'd observed through her wolf.

Over another slow sip of scotch, she pictured a book on the front table of her local bookstore with an artist's rendering of Kate on the cover. The journals contained the material she needed. Flush with descriptions of the wolf's feelings, her attachments, her drives—she could use them to give others a glimpse into the intimacies she'd shared, to craft a memorial that could give her girl a measure of justice. Or, at least, a version of immortality. Better she do so, from love, than leave it to Chilson-Reed with their tacky virtual realities. She tapped out a quick response: *Of course I'd be interested. Let me get a proposal together!*

On her laptop screen, gusts of wind blew the snow in a swirling dance. Sean bent to grab her journals from the floor. She missed the passage of a gaunt creature through the border trees—the flash of its stare catching the moonlight, floating like a starving ghost.

ACKNOWLEDGMENTS

My sign-off for *Feed Them Silence* has to begin with the most obvious acknowledgment of all: this novella was drafted during the earliest months of full-scale pandemic isolation in the United States. At the time, I was enrolled in a spring graduate seminar through the University of Kentucky's Social Theory program where faculty from multiple departments come together to co-teach on a central theme . . . which was, in our case, animals. In hindsight, the timing was awfully exquisite. No one could've guessed that, for example, our final guest scholar—who researched microbial and viral life—would be forced to cancel so she could focus on COVID-19. But even then, in January 2020, those of us with friends and family overseas were already consuming news of spreading illness with white-knuckled terror.

And of course, shit proceeded to go south fast.

Governmental and private-sector failures to effectively respond dug the entire world further, and further, and *further* into an ongoing mass death catastrophe. I remember spinning out gruesome policy predictions with colleagues, then watching them come true one by one. Late capitalism dictating the precise *worth* of a life, to be preserved or destroyed, based on the logic of markets. Upsurges in the severity and violence of anti-Asian racism and xenophobia, which trickles down through supposedly progressive spaces like universities as well. And later, vaccine access locked through corporate patents though their research had been pursued with public funds. All of the supremely goddamn depressing seminar research readings began to coalesce as I locked down, entirely alone, in a tiny cavernesque apartment.

Feed Them Silence grew from that fertile, toxic soil. Ultimately, the novella wrestles with the fears and worries of a singular moment in time—but the emotions and critiques at its core remain, I hope, prescient. I'm sure plenty of other artists will be scribbling their way through closing notes like these over the next decade or more.

* * *

As for acknowledgments proper, I've got to first send boundless affection to the people who care for me on the daily: Brett, Dave, Em, Emilie, and Trisha, among others. Through hours upon hours of Zoom calls, screen-share scary movie nights, and offering my single ass a cozy domestic pod through months of isolation: without you, there wouldn't be enough of *me* left to make any art at all. Thanks are also owed to my mother for helping me keep fed, as well as the friends and colleagues at the University of Kentucky who've made the ongoing doctoral process more bearable. And to keep the trend going: thanks to the members of BTS for your artistic, political, and emotional contributions to my life.

Special thank-you to the faculty whose seminar spawned *Feed Them Silence*: Erin Koch, Doug Slaymaker, and Tony Stallins. Their readings, conversations, and openness to receiving a piece of fiction as a term project—in a critical social theory seminar, oops—gave me room to chase down a burst of grim inspiration. Thanks as well to Christine Marran, whose campus visit came right before the seminar shifted online due to the pandemic. Our breakfast conversation on Ursula K. Le Guin's fiction, global circulations of culture, and the ethical dimensions of storytelling was a real delight. If I'd known it would be the last scholar interview I'd do face to face for the next two plus years, I'd have taken better notes.

Flinging further gratitude toward all of the arts communities whose critiques, affections, checks and balances, and group chats sustain me. There's the crew of Kentucky writers (though some of their bodies now settle elsewhere) who offered feedback on early drafts: Alex Head, Alix E. Harrow, Ashley Blooms, Christopher Rowe, Elizabeth Kilcoyne, Gwenda Bond, Olivia Sailor, Sam Milligan, and Z Jackson. Then, there's the wonderful denizens of the Bunker! Thanks for workshopping the title with me, because continuing to call it "the wolf book" wasn't going to hold water for much longer. And thanks also for your bountiful patience when I get on a roll about things like "tweets I really shouldn't have read" or "academic books wherein my enthusiasm outweighs general interest" (or my uncontrollable urge to repost thirst-trap shots of Wonho for everyone to see).

Thanks once more to my agent, Tara Gilbert, for handling the fiddly contractual bits—especially given that I wrote a novella that very much *wasn't* the novella I originally proposed. But the biggest of thanks as always for the entire Tordotcom team, whose myriad labors are the reason *Feed Them Silence* exists. Starting with Carl Engle-Laird, my editor: your engaged, critical feedback always helps craft a stronger, sexier, sharper book. My endless gratitude for Irene Gallo, Christina Orlando, Matt Rusin, Libby Collins, Sarah Pannenberg, Eileen Lawrence, Michael Dudding, Jordan Hanley, Sam Friedlander, Christine Foltzer, FORT Studio, Steven Bucsok, Dakota Griffin, NaNá Stoelzle, and Kyle Avery.

Last but far from least: thanks to the reader about to flip the back cover of this novella shut. Couldn't do any of this without you.